CHAOS EVOLVES

HARLEY TATE

ISBN: 9781973259381

CHAOS EVOLVES

A POST-APOCALYPTIC SURVIVAL THRILLER

A month into the apocalypse, would you still be alive?

Colt survived an emergency landing, a standoff with a rogue militia, and more than his share of bullets. With the threat of danger around every corner, leaving the city is his only choice. But with seven people relying on him, Colt discovers the forest is deadlier than the streets.

If you lose everything, can you summon the strength to go on?

As the city fades into the distance, Dani hopes her luck is changing. But a catastrophic accident turns everything upside down. Grief-stricken and desperate, she must summon the strength to carry on, even when the odds—and her friends—are stacked against her.

The end of the world brings out the best and worst in all of us.

Starvation, dehydration, and danger lurk behind every tree. If Colt, Dani, and the rest of their group can't put tragedy behind them, it might be the end of their journey. With guilt and anguish tearing them apart, an unexpected visitor becomes their only hope.

The EMP is only the beginning.

Chaos Gains is book six in the *After the EMP* series, a post-apocalyptic thriller series following ordinary people trying to survive after a geomagnetic storm destroys the nation's power grid.

Subscribe to Harley's newsletter and receive an exclusive companion short story, *Darkness Falls*, absolutely free.

www.harleytate.com/subscribe

* * *

THIRTY DAYS WITHOUT POWER

CHAPTER ONE

DANI

250 Bellwether Street
Eugene, Oregon
8:00 a.m.

"Naw, man. That SOB kept his stash under the counter. I know it."

Dani crouched behind a tipped-over rack of Funyuns and held her breath. The two men rooting through the convenience store were too busy looking for drugs to notice her so far. But kicking one empty can or stepping on an empty chip bag and she could be their runner-up target.

She shifted her weight, hoping they would find whatever they were looking for and get the hell out. If she didn't get back to the apartment soon, Colt would come looking. She didn't need his worry.

"There ain't nothin' here but some nudie mags,

Carl. You done wasted my time." The heavyset guy with a stained T-shirt and Ducks ball cap lumbered around the counter. He bent down with a grunt of effort and snatched up a Slim Jim. He tore it open with his teeth and spit the plastic wrapper on the floor. "Let's git before the rain starts up again. I don't wanna hike it home in the wet."

The guy named Carl banged around behind the counter, his stringy blond head popping up now and then to glance around like a chipmunk too far from his burrow. "Just give me a minute, will ya? I know it's around here somewhere."

The fat guy grumbled and leaned against an empty cooler as he chomped on the meat stick. Even across the store, Dani could hear his teeth grinding together and lips smacking with greasy effort. She fought back a wave of nausea.

Carl whooped and his fist shot up, a wrinkled plastic baggie in his hand. "I told you, Rocky. I told you!" He jumped up, beaming in delight. "It's all here. Got to be fifteen dubs, man."

Dani swallowed down her disgust. Thanks to her mother's vice, she knew more about the street than she ever wanted to know. If these two idiots were only after a few bags of pot, they were small time. Not a serious threat. Her shoulders eased as she sucked in a full breath.

Carl made his way to Rocky, holding the bag in front of him like a kid with a full Christmas stocking. "See? Darlene will go ape-shit for this, won't she?"

Rocky shrugged. "Shit if I know man. Let's go."

They left together, Carl with a bounce in his step and Rocky with a heavy swagger due more to his weight than his ego.

Dani counted to five hundred after their shapes disappeared from view before moving. In the last five days, she'd run across three times as many rats as people, but that didn't mean plenty of people weren't out there. Most of the stores were ransacked—cleared out of beer and snacks and stupid stuff that used to hold value. Even the liquor store windows grimaced with broken shards of glass in front of empty shelves.

Before the EMP, Dani often thought that living with her mother in this downtrodden, sad-sack part of town was the bottom of the barrel. She'd been wrong. Take the same area and flick off the lights and it only sank lower, right through the floor to the dark depths beyond.

Now the sagging storefronts gaped like the maws of death and the only people still around roamed the streets without regard for the prior rule of law. It was every girl for herself.

Dani tugged open her backpack and scooped up every unopened package of chips and cookies she could find, dumping Tastycake chocolate brownies and Hostess Sno Balls on top of chili cheese Fritos and bags of Takis. Would she ever see a piece of fresh fruit or a vegetable again? Not that they'd been high on her list of food choices, but she'd at least seen a salad in the school cafeteria five days a week.

Would lettuce ever surface in the town of Eugene? Or would everyone be relegated to scrounging for canned peaches and green beans to ward off scurvy?

Was scurvy even a thing or just something Gran used in the face of a plate full of broccoli? There was so much Dani didn't know.

She shook off the spiraling thoughts and tugged her bag up onto her shoulder. Colt had admonished her to look for more than just snacks, so she set to exploring the edges of the store. Bleach, batteries, and baby wipes. Those were the key items on her list.

It didn't take long to find the baby wipes; no one on this side of town gave a crap about kids. Dani shoved three containers into her bag and tried to fit a fourth, but it kept popping out the top. Darn it. She shuffled through the debris and broken shelves to the counter where Carl found the bag of pot. She tugged a white shopping bag with a bright red smiley face off the rack and fluffed it open.

"Have a Nice Day," it proclaimed on the other side.

Yeah, right.

She shoved the baby wipes into the bag and turned around. A display of candy caught her eye. Most of the chocolate was gone, but a bag of Werther's Originals still hung from the metal post. Gran's favorite candy. Dani reached for the bag as memories of Gran's candy bowl filled her mind.

She choked back a sudden sob.

If only Gran had told her about the cancer, they could have done something about it before it was too late. She tore the bag open and pulled out a shiny foil-wrapped candy. Gran only let her have one on special occasions. A birthday. A good grade on a test. Dani unwrapped the hard little caramel and popped it into her mouth.

Butter and sugar and the taste of Gran's love. Emotion clogged her throat. She gagged and spit the candy on the floor. "Get it together, Dani. You don't have time for this."

"Talkin' to yourself? I heard that's the first sign you've gone crazy."

Dani spun around. *Oh, no.* Her lips edged into a phony smile. "Hi, Skeeter."

"That's all I get? The world goes to shit and all you can say is hi?" Skeeter slinked inside, all smarm and sleaze. His faded cords hung loose on his hips and the chain connecting a wallet to his belt jingled as he moved. He glided past the candy wrappers and crushed bags of chips like a snake in muddy water.

Dani held out the bag. "Candy?"

With bony fingers, Skeeter plucked the entire bag from Dani's grip and fished a single candy out. He held it out to her like he'd done her a favor. "Where's your mother? She owes me for a Q."

Dani's eyes went wide as she took the candy. Skeeter gave her a quarter ounce? That cost two hundred dollars before. Now that the power went out, the price of heroin had to skyrocket. She couldn't believe Skeeter would give up that much without payment. "You never front her that much."

Skeeter grinned, accentuating the hollows of his cheeks. "Your old lady made it worth my while, if you catch my drift." He unwrapped one of the candies and popped it in his mouth as his eyes lingered in places they shouldn't. "You ever consider following in your mother's footsteps? With a body like that, you'd fetch a mint."

Dani backtracked until she bumped the display behind her.

Skeeter laughed. "Don't get all wide-eyed and skittish, girl. I ain't gonna force ya. My clients like 'em able and willing." He rolled his hips and sucked on the candy and Dani pressed her lips together. Skeeter had always been decent to her, despite pumping her mother full of drugs. But how would he react when he learned her mother had moved on to greener pastures?

She played it off. "I think she's on a bender."

"How about you try that again."

Dani hesitated. "What do you mean?"

"No dealer in this 'hood will give your momma another dime. She's in hock to all of us."

"How bad?"

"As bad as it gets." Skeeter stepped close enough to reach out and stroke Dani's hair. She forced her body still. "You and me, we have an understanding, but some of these other guys… Let's just say they won't be so accommodating. You tell Becky if she doesn't pay up, her daughter's gonna have to work it off. One way or another."

Dani swallowed. "I'll tell her."

"Good." Skeeter stepped back and shook the bag of Werther's. "Thanks for the candy, babe. You've always been a sweetheart."

He sauntered from the store, leaving unease and fear in his wake. Dani couldn't pay off all the dealers in the neighborhood. Nor could she tell them where to find her mother. No one would believe that her mother had wormed her way into the militia's good graces.

Dani shoved the single candy in her pocket and looked around. If she'd been on her own, now would be the time to leave town. But she wasn't alone.

Not only did she have Colt to think about, but the Wilkinses and the Harpers, too. If Harvey hadn't dragged a dying Colt to safety, Dani would be sitting in a makeshift jail cell at the University of Oregon, waiting for the militia who controlled the area to decide her fate.

If Melody hadn't covered for her when the militia shot up Harvey's house, she would be a pile of ash in the burned-out remains of the entire block. Dani owed them her life and Colt's, too. Now, because they risked everything to save her and Colt, they were homeless and scared and unsure what to do.

She couldn't abandon them, no matter the danger.

Everyone was hungry and dirty and exhausted. Melody almost died. Doug and Larkin and Colt killed more militia members than Dani could count. Even Will suffered. If it hadn't been for Dani and Colt stumbling into their lives, none of this would have happened. She owed it to them to help.

Dani grabbed her backpack and shopping bag and took a deep breath. No matter the risk, she had to keep scavenging. There were three more stores on her list to clear and she wouldn't go home until she'd done it. No turning back. Not now. Not ever.

CHAPTER TWO

MELODY

489 BELLWETHER STREET
    Eugene, Oregon
    8:30 a.m.

"COME ON, YOU STUPID THING." MELODY WRESTLED THE shower curtain to one side. The fresh rainwater sloshed and she bit back a curse. *I can't spill this.* She took a calming breath and tried again, tugging the edge of the curtain toward the waiting two-liter bottle with both hands.

The water rolled toward her like a rising tide and she struggled to keep the plastic steady. Water splashed over the edge and down into the bottle anchored between her feet. As it filled, she sucked in a much-needed breath of air.

So far, so good. The first bottle filled and she pulled up

on the plastic curtain to stop the flow. *Only four more to go.*
The makeshift water collection station Colt rigged up on
the edge of the patio had done the job. Now they had
enough water for a few days.

Melody pushed a greasy clump of hair off her face
and pulled over the next bottle, filling it without so
much as a spilled drop. The more she worked, the
better she got, until at last, every bottle sat full and the
plastic curtain held nothing more than a splash
of water.

She leaned back and exhaled. If only the sky would
rain hot coffee and half-and-half. After screwing the
caps on each bottle, she carted them into the apartment.
Thanks to the rainy weather of the past few days and
the trash full of empty bottles throughout the apartment
building, they managed to collect almost ten gallons
of water.

It wasn't close to enough.

In the past, survival had always been an abstract
concept for Melody. Even after the grid failed, with the
National Guard carting in water and food, she hadn't
gone hungry. Sure, the pit toilet in the backyard stunk,
but she'd been able to wash and eat and sleep in her
own bed.

Now, though, the horror of the future had truly set
in. No water. No food. No shelter. Nothing they didn't
fight for or scrounge up from some rat-infested hole in
the wall. She scratched her dirty scalp and frowned.
Would it ever get better than this?

"Staring at those bottles won't turn them into coffee,
honey."

Melody smiled as Gloria walked past her into the kitchen. "I'd settle for an ice-cold shower, to be honest."

Gloria poured herself a glass of water and motioned toward the empty patio. She eased into a chair opposite Gloria and focused on the horizon. Three miles away, Colonel Jarvis had electricity and hot water and enough rations to last for months.

They didn't have enough food for the day.

The first pangs of hunger hit her stomach and Melody glanced back inside. Everyone was either gone or still sleeping. She and Gloria were alone.

At over twice Melody's age, Gloria Wilkins had seen her fair share of hardship, but this had to be the worst. She caught her former neighbor's eye. "Do you regret it?"

The wrinkles deepened around Gloria's mouth. "Leaving? After our house burned to the ground we didn't have much choice."

"No. I meant all of it. Taking in Colt and Dani. Standing up to Jarvis." Her voice cracked and Melody took a moment to swallow. "Everything."

"Not for a second. How can you even ask that after what those men tried to do?"

Melody focused on a crumbling patch of stucco on the wall. She hadn't been able to sleep since she killed that horrible man. Nightmares of what he wanted… the things he said…. She hugged herself even though she wasn't cold. "If we hadn't taken Colt and Dani in, none of that would have happened."

"Colt didn't do those things. Jarvis and his militia did. Don't blame the people helping us."

"I'm not." Melody risked a glance at the older woman. She'd tried to keep the what-ifs at bay the last few days, but as every angry bruise faded to yellowed skin, she wondered. "I can't help thinking: what if we'd minded our own business?"

Gloria blew out a puff of breath. "It might have delayed everything a little, but sooner or later, the militia would have come for us."

"Why? We were following the rules." As the last word slipped out, Lottie trotted up, hungry little eyes begging for breakfast. Melody frowned. "Okay, maybe not all the rules. But they wouldn't have burned down our houses over Lottie."

"You don't know that." Gloria smoothed back her gray hair. "Look at what they did to you, Melody. That room with the beds and the gaudy clothes and the line of men outside the door…" Gloria shuddered. "They were going to use you no matter what." She shook her head. "All the people like me with nothing to offer— those are ones I worry about. How long will they live under Jarvis's control? How long will he let them drain his resources before he puts a bullet in their heads?"

Melody jerked away. Gloria was right. Jarvis didn't care about a single resident of Eugene. She remembered how Lucas's blood splattered the walls when Jarvis shot him in the head. Angela's face, contorted in terror before Jarvis's minions killed her.

Still, Melody couldn't help but mourn. They had spent five days scrubbing and cleaning and organizing the top-floor apartment she now sat in, but it wasn't home. Jarvis burned their houses to the ground. Every memento. Every treasure she kept from her parents, gone up in smoke and ash. Her family home, destroyed because of what?

Because the power went out?

It didn't seem real. If it weren't for the bruises and cuts all over her body, she would be tempted to call it all a dream. Some twisted nightmare she couldn't wake up from. But the wounds were real. Melody pushed up the sleeve of her shirt and stared at the finger marks now yellowing across her arm.

When they weren't cleaning the apartment, they had worked countless hours clearing and fortifying the building. Between the barricades in the front and the boobytraps in the back, she felt secure from a thief or an enterprising addict. But not the militia. Not after she'd seen what they could do.

She spoke the thoughts forcing their way to the surface. "If our experience is anything to go by, Jarvis won't hesitate to eliminate the dead weight."

"Who are you calling dead weight?"

Major James Larkin's jubilant voice filled the apartment and Melody glanced up. He lumbered out to the patio, arms laden with plastic grocery bags.

"Busy morning shopping?"

He set the bags on the coffee table and fluffed one open. "Straight from the finest gourmet market in the Pacific Northwest. I present, breakfast!" His hands emerged with a crushed box of Pop Tarts and a partial six-pack of Mountain Dew.

"Oh, my, what rare and exotic delicacies." Melody

snorted, but her mood lightened. "Where on earth did you find them?"

Larkin fell onto the seat next to her with a sigh. "Top-floor apartment three blocks over. It's getting harder and harder to scavenge, that's for sure."

Melody took the box and tugged it open. Two wrapped packages still inside. She handed one to him. "Here, you should eat."

He shook his head. "Ladies first, I insist."

Melody frowned, but handed it over to Gloria all the same. "I should go next time. It's not fair that you and Colt are doing most of the work."

"You're injured. You need time to rest."

"It's been five days. I can help."

"Tell that to Colt. If he had his way, you'd be locked up here permanently."

Melody pulled a Mountain Dew free from the plastic holding the cans together. "He doesn't get to make that decision." She popped the top of the can and took a sip. "Ugh. This stuff still takes like pee."

"You do know that's why it's yellow, right?" Melody's brother Doug laughed as he walked out to join them on the patio. He shook hands with Larkin and sat down. "That joke never gets old."

Melody rolled her eyes. "It does when you've heard it for almost twenty years."

"Ouch. I think she just called you old." Larkin pulled a soda off the plastic and handed it to Doug. "Is she always so mean?"

Doug grinned. "Only to her brother."

She pouted. "I didn't drink Mountain Dew for years because of you. And I still can't get over the taste."

She still remembered the day Doug poured the contents of a can on the sidewalk and let his sister in on the secret. He'd leaned over, his twelve-year-old frame still lanky with youth, and whispered about how a guy peed into every can.

Melody barked out a laugh, her vocal cords unused to the effort. She stroked her throat. Had it been that long since she'd relaxed?

Gloria handed over a Pop Tart and Melody took it with a grateful smile. Doug and Larkin split the other package. The four of them chomped and slurped like a group of college kids on break between classes. They had done an amazing job turning the abandoned apartment into a place eight people and a little dog could call home, but she knew they couldn't stay.

As soon as everyone healed enough to hit the road, they would drive out of Eugene and never look back. The more miles they put between themselves, Colonel Jarvis, and the militia he controlled, the better. Part of her wished they could launch an attack and kill the man, but that was the stuff of movies. No more real than an action-hero film.

She scooped Lottie up into her arms and broke off a piece of the pastry. Lottie nibbled on it and relaxed into Melody's lap. Maybe Colt and Dani would have more success scavenging. At some point their luck had to change.

CHAPTER THREE

COLT

672 Bellwether Street
    Eugene, Oregon
    9:00 a.m.

Colt eased into the living room with his Sig Sauer level and ready. Greasy rivulets of rain and grime obscured the morning sun through the window. He clicked on a flashlight and panned the space. *Empty.*

The stink of decaying garbage hit his nose and he snorted. No one cleaned up around here. He cleared the room before ducking into the hall and surveying the bathroom and bedroom. No one stuck around, either. As he holstered his weapon, Colt took stock.

Another abandoned apartment on the wrong side of town, another sad sack of existence wiped out because an EMP fried the grid. Power kept so many people hanging on by a thread. Wreck it and they flat out couldn't make it.

Clothes littered the bedroom floor, cast-off jeans and shirts discarded like so many others. He sidestepped the largest piles and stopped in front of a dresser.

A single photo frame sat on top. Cheap metal, plastic instead of glass. A kid smiling with a mouth full of holes instead of teeth, ratty hair yanked back in a ponytail, faded clothes, and bare feet. Big, brown eyes still full of hope. He glanced around.

Not a single toy or stuffed animal. The kid couldn't live there. He tugged open the top drawer of the dresser: men's underwear and mismatched socks. A bachelor pad.

Colt rooted through the drawers and pulled out a pair of jeans and a few T-shirts. They would fit Will or Harvey without a doubt.

He slipped a backpack off his shoulders and stuffed the clothes inside before heading to the bathroom. With a quick unzip, Colt added his own piss to the moldy mess inside the toilet bowl. He'd taken to using whatever abandoned space suited him best. One less worry to deal with back at the apartment.

It had been five days since they escaped the patrolled areas of the city and Jarvis's control. Five days since the lights of the University lit up and turned everyone's attention straight to campus.

Since then, the streets emptied. Even in the fringes where they now lived, almost everyone was gone. Barely any dealers. Only a handful of strung-out addicts hanging on thanks to pills or booze. The glow of the lights attracted everyone else like insects to a nighttime barbecue.

He hit the kitchen and opened the cabinets one at a time, looking for anything they could use. The doors squeaked in protest and Colt came up empty. Nothing but dishes and dust.

They didn't need glassware. They needed food.

Colt thought about Colonel Jarvis and the men under his command. From everything they had seen and the stories Larkin told, the National Guardsmen who stayed loyal to Jarvis were a full-blown militia. A thousand men, at least, with a psychopath in command. Thanks to their systematic inspections, the militia controlled not just the University of Oregon, but most of Eugene. Only the bad parts of town had been left to rot.

He closed his eyes and relived the moment when he had Jarvis in his sights. A single shot and the militia would have dissolved into chaos. One bullet and they wouldn't be rooting through forgotten apartments for supplies. The Harpers and Wilkinses would be safe. Secure.

But he didn't take the shot. Colt made the choice to save Dani instead. Now they were barely hanging on while Jarvis lived it up on the University campus with electricity and water and food. Every night he dreamt about sneaking back to campus and finishing the job. But he didn't stand a chance against a thousand soldiers with orders to kill on sight. Walking away from Jarvis would be the hardest thing Colt had ever done.

Harder than leaving a mission unfinished. Harder

than following orders to stand down when he could take the shot. As a SEAL, he didn't have a choice. He followed orders, no matter his opinion. Hell, he worked at not having an opinion most of the time.

But this was different. The choice to walk away was all his and he couldn't change it now. No Blackhawks would swoop in and bend the grass as troops jumped out. No backup forces would come along behind and clear the college. Colt was on his own. To survive, he would have to let Jarvis own Eugene.

Colt shook off the spiraling thoughts and crouched in front of the sink cabinet. As he tugged open the doors, a roach scurried past his foot. Colt ignored it and poked around, hoping for something more than disappointment.

A half-empty jug of bleach was the only reward. *Better than nothing.* He shoved it in his backpack and stood up. So far, he'd cleared five of the twelve apartments in the building and all he had to show for it was a handful of clothes and a bottle of bleach.

He eased back to the front door and tugged it open. And froze. Was that the door or something else? He swore the hinges opened without a squeak the first time. Colt eased the door shut. Silence.

Definitely not the door. He spun in a slow arc, checking for hostiles inside the apartment. No flutter of fabric or creak of floor. No flash of hair or glimpse of skin behind the couch.

He pulled his gun and held it pointed at the floor. The warped linoleum groaned as he passed the kitchen, and Colt paused at the edge of the living room. A voice

in his head whispered to leave. Just forget whoever was
hiding in that godforsaken slum and move on. But a
threat was a threat.

Where hadn't he checked? He crouched to peer
beneath the couch. Nothing but roach carcasses and
dirt. He glanced in the tight space behind the massive
tube TV. Empty.

Colt eased into the bedroom once again. The
mattress sagged on the floor, dingy sheets piled in a mess
on top. The dresser hugged the wall. He approached the
closet. Gun drawn, ready. The door protested and Colt
jerked, hard.

Brought his gun up, pointed it into the dark.
Nothing visible. He flicked on his flashlight. The space
went back farther than it seemed. A walk-in. He panned
the light.

Hanging racks that should have held shoes or
blankets obscured his view. They hung in tatters, holes
on the bottom, frayed edges. A balled-up towel gave
substance to one sagging shelf.

Colt reached for the closest one and caught a
glimpse of movement.

"Out!" He pulled back and brought up his Sig,
aiming at the space behind the fabric shelves. "Out or
I'll shoot."

A keening wail sounded from the darkness, high-
pitched and wild. Was it an animal? A stray dog or cat?
Hungry pets could turn deadly. He reached out and
gripped the fabric in his fist. Yanked it clean off the rod.

The creature scrunching into the corner wasn't a
dog or a cat. At one point, it had been a child. Hair

hung in matted clumps around her face. A fairy peeked out from behind a layer of dirt and stains on her nightgown. Bruises covered her visible skin.

She blinked and squirmed under the harsh flashlight beam, holding her hands out in front of her to block the light. Her fingernails were ripped and torn, crusted with blood and dirt.

Colt eased the circle of light closer to the floor. The child lowered her hands and opened her eyes. Big, brown eyes. The girl from the photo.

He lowered the gun. "It's okay. I won't hurt you."

She squeaked out a whimper.

"Are you here alone?" Colt eased down into a crouch, remembering from somewhere that kids felt less threatened when grown-ups came down to their level.

The child nodded. *Shit*. Had she been here for the entire month? That explained the complete lack of food and general filth. But how had she managed to get by? If she lived there with her father, where was he? Colt glanced behind him. From everything he'd seen, no adult still lived there.

There would be some evidence surely; a cigarette, food wrappers, empty beer bottles or cans. Something.

He glanced back at the girl. She still crouched in the corner with her knees pinned to her chest, willing her body to disappear. For once in his life, Colt didn't know what to do. He couldn't leave her there, filthy and starving. Someone without a conscience could find the girl next. But he couldn't bring her back to the apartment, either. They already had too many mouths to feed and she didn't look willing.

Colt dug into his pocket and pulled out half a piece of beef jerky. The last of his breakfast. He held it out. The child's eyes went wide. Her tiny nostrils flared.

She leaned forward and dropped her knees to the side. Her mouth opened, words tumbled out in a whisper. Colt leaned forward. "What was that? I can't hear you."

Again she mumbled, too quiet and indistinct to understand. Colt thrust the hunk of dried meat toward her. She grabbed it with a grubby hand and shoved the whole thing in her mouth.

"Sorry."

The second Colt processed the single, distorted word, he spun away from the closet. It was too late. Wood grain flooded his vision and the crack of a bat against his skull knocked him to the floor.

CHAPTER FOUR

COLT

672 BELLWETHER STREET
   Eugene, Oregon
   11:00 a.m.

THE PAIN WOKE HIM UP. A CONSTANT THUMPING walloped his head as if a jackhammer splintered his skull. He reached for his head, but his hands didn't make it more than an inch. Something tacky and thick pulled at his skin and arm hair.

"Grrrnn." The sound rumbling up from his chest was half word, half grunt. His tongue took up his entire mouth and his spit stuck like hardening cement. Maybe the jackhammer was drilling in the wrong place.

He blinked, but the world refused to cooperate. Splashes of white and blue rushed by like the scenery on a carnival ride. *Christ*. He closed his eyes and focused on breathing.

In. Out. In. Out.

The tilt-a-whirl of his brain slowed. The nausea threatening to heave up his paltry breakfast receded. *What the hell happened to me?*

Colt opened his eyes and the room didn't spin.

Now he knew why all he could smell was piss. He sat on a toilet, hands duct taped to the seat. A sink clung to the wall opposite his face. He leaned forward and his forehead melted against the cool porcelain. The throbbing eased and he took stock.

A tub caked in dirt sagged on his left. No shower curtain. Nowhere to hide.

The window above the tub showed promise. Two by two with frosted glass that looked too old to be double-paned. If he knocked out all the glass, he might fit. He thought it over. Fifty-fifty odds. Might get stuck halfway.

He swiveled his head to the right, forehead pressed against the sink. The door to the room was wedged tight into the frame a few feet away.

He gave his hands a tug. They didn't budge.

Colt closed his eyes and tried to remember. *How did I get here?* He thought back through the morning. Leaving for a scavenging mission, hitting apartment building after apartment building and coming up empty. The kid in the closet.

His eyes popped open. She'd been bait. Plain and simple.

And I fell for it. Colt cursed himself and yanked on

the tape. *I've gone soft.* A few days with normal people who didn't understand the current state of affairs and look what happened. When he walked out of the University of Oregon, he'd been a free man on his own. No one to hold him back. No one to affect his decisions.

Then he rescued Dani. Every decision after that point had been with her in mind. He didn't leave. He didn't disappear into the wilderness like he'd planned. No. He'd gone and made himself a family.

Was she a burden? Yes and no. She understood the way the world worked now, maybe more than anyone. And Colt cared for her. She'd become the closest thing to a daughter he'd ever get. If he'd stuck with just her… If they'd left town at the first opportunity…

Harvey and Gloria and Will would have a home. Melody wouldn't have suffered at the hands of Jarvis and his men. Hell, Larkin would still be following orders. All because Colt didn't follow his gut and leave.

He tugged again on the tape and it rolled against his skin, tightening its grip. Rocking back and forth, he tried to loosen the glue, but it held fast, ripping out the hair around his wrist, but not yielding an inch.

Colt thought about everything his new companions suffered because of him: the fire that destroyed the Wilkins and Harper homes, Gloria and Melody's kidnapping, their abuse at the hands of Jarvis and his men. For all that he wanted to take Dani and run, he couldn't. He owed these people a safe place. He couldn't leave them until they were secure and capable of fending for themselves.

They saved his life. Dani's too. Colt couldn't turn his back on them. Not now.

He sat up and braced his feet on the floor. With a deep breath, he rose up, straining against the tape and the toilet. The seat wobbled. He pulled harder, grimacing against the tension in his arms and the heat and pain surrounding his wrists.

Nothing.

Sagging back against the toilet, he sucked in a frustrated breath. With a grunt against the discomfort, Colt twisted his upper body and inspected the tape. It wrapped around each of his wrists at least three times, around the toilet seat, and then all the way down to the base of the toilet. Whoever secured him took their time.

Colt thought about what he knew.

It had been a single man's apartment. A bachelor pad, despite the kid in the closet. Was he still in the same place? He thought back to clearing the bathroom and glanced up. The same broken shade covered the single bulb in the ceiling.

I haven't been moved.

He didn't know if that was good or bad. It could mean there was only one adult and a kid to worry about. But counting on that would be foolish. There could be twenty people waiting on the other side of the bathroom door. Colt shifted on the seat and frowned.

They took everything. His gun. His backup knife in his right pocket. His wallet. The bags he'd carried. By now they knew who he was and what he was up to. If the militia was involved…

Damn it.

He tugged on the tape again, but it was hopeless. Unless he found a way to rip the toilet off the floor, he wasn't getting out of there without help. He had to hope that whoever hit him upside the head and taped him up wasn't in with Colonel Jarvis. Best case scenario, he could sweet talk his way out of there. Worst case, this might be the last resting place of Colt Potter.

Leaning back, he closed his eyes. He couldn't do anything about his current predicament. Rest was the best option in a hostage situation. The more he could conserve his energy, the better he could take on whatever came next.

There would be an opportunity and he needed to be ready for it.

Colt startled awake some time later. Something plinked against his cheek and he jerked back. Found the source. Scowled.

"Get out."

The little girl from the closet stood in the open bathroom door, popping little candies in her mouth one after the other. Her matted hair hung in her face and her grubby little toes dug into the dirt on the floor. She was filthy. Worse than a street urchin or a runaway. But she smirked at him like the richest little princess.

"I said, get out."

She wiggled against the door frame, but didn't leave. "Daddy says I ain't supposed to listen to you." She pointed a neon green candy at him. "You're a bad man."

Colt managed to keep his expression vacant and even. "Tell your dad I want to speak with him."

She eyed him with the same brown eyes that pulled on his heart in the closet. "No."

"Why not?"

"Because." She shook the bag in her little fist and poured out a pile of candy before shoving them all in her mouth. Her cheeks swelled like a chipmunk. As she chewed, rainbow spit leaked from her lips and dribbled down her chin.

He flexed his hands, gave the tape a tug. It wasn't going anywhere. He needed a new plan. After staring at the girl's faded nightgown and the sleeves that barely reached mid-forearm, he glanced up. Smiled. "So what's your dad like? Is he nice to you?"

The little girl stopped chewing and wiped her face with her dirty sleeve. "Sometimes."

"What happens when he's not nice?"

She fidgeted with the bag of candy and glanced in the hall. "I get locked in the closet."

"Is that why you were in there when I found you? Because your daddy wasn't nice?"

"Maybe." She glanced at the hallway again.

"If you come over here and help me with this tape, I can protect you. Your dad can't hurt you if I'm free."

She wavered, her whole body swaying first toward him, then away.

A little more convincing, and she might be his ticket out of there. Colt grinned even broader. "I've got a daughter, she's not that much older than you. I bet the two of you would really hit it off."

The little girl's face closed up, the wide, curious stare

replaced with a tight frown. "No. Daddy wouldn't like it."

"He doesn't have to know. It could be our secret."

She focused on the wrinkled, almost-empty candy bag.

"I've got a lot more candy back at my place. And food and water, too. You could come stay for a while. Eat all you wanted."

The bag rustled in her hand.

"How about you just loosen this tape a little bit and I do the rest?"

She rose up onto the balls of her feet, but didn't take a step.

Colt bit back the words of frustration on his tongue. The girl was his best chance. He couldn't wreck it. Colt managed another smile. "My name's Colt. What's yours?"

She opened her mouth as another voice called out. "My girl knows better than to tell a stranger her name. Ain't that right, sweetheart?"

CHAPTER FIVE

DANI

489 Bellwether Street
   Eugene, Oregon
   11:00 a.m.

"What do you mean he's not back?" Dani paced the length of the faded living room. "Where did he go?"

Larkin shrugged. "North. He planned on hitting the last apartments on Bellwether before it turned completely commercial."

Dani chewed on her thumbnail until it splintered. "There's nothing up there. All those places are full of addicts and crazies. Half of them rent by the day."

As soon as she walked in the door after clearing her portion of the street, Dani went searching for Colt. First, she checked the balcony where the Wilkins family sat staring out at the south side of town and their old street. Then she eased into the hall and peeked in the bedrooms. Doug slept on a bed shoved against the wall, his boot-clad feet dangling off the edge, but all the others were empty.

No sign of Colt.

It wasn't until she'd interrupted Larkin and Melody's debate about personal hygiene and the status of the city sewers that anyone noticed Colt's absence. Now they were blowing it off like he'd decided to take the long way home after work.

Larkin stretched before leaning back against the couch. "I wouldn't worry. Colt can take care of himself."

She cut him a glance. "He's never late."

The soldier didn't know Colt like Dani did. Sure, Larkin and Colt spent time at a military hospital together years ago, but Larkin hadn't survived a burning building or jumped three stories to safety with Colt. Dani knew the man like no one else. Even if he'd found a reason to delay, he'd have come home, explained, and gone back out. He wouldn't blow a deadline.

Maybe it was the way she stared Larkin down or the edge of anger in her voice, but at last, he threw her a bone. "If Colt doesn't show in the next few hours, we can assemble a team and check it out."

Dani shook her head. "Not good enough. Colt needs help now. In a few hours it could be too late."

"Don't you think you're overreacting?" Melody spoke up for the first time since Dani interrupted. With her hair pulled back in a ponytail, the bruises across her cheek and neck stood out in angry blotches. Of all people, Melody should understand the risks of leaving Colt to fend for himself. Captain Ferguson almost killed her, but she thought Dani was overreacting?

"What if Colt said the same thing after you disappeared? What if he waited for a few hours to rescue you?"

Melody opened her mouth, but shut it just as fast. Her hand lingered on her still-healing ankle as she glanced at Larkin. That's it? No acknowledgment of the truth? No, *Gee, Dani, I guess you're right?*

I should knock their heads together. She plucked a rifle off the battered coffee table and slung it over her shoulder.

If Melody wasn't going to support her, then the heck with it. Dani didn't have time to convince her or Larkin of the potential danger. Colt needed help and Dani planned to give it. "I'm going to find him before it's too late."

"Colt's a big boy, he can get himself out of a jam."

Dani refused to look at Larkin as she tightened the laces on her dirty kicks. "You don't know what some of the people around here are like. A month without a fix? If any addicts are still alive, they're out of their minds with cravings. They could do anything."

She thought about some of the worst days with her mother when they didn't have any money and her mother could only think about how to score. Lies. Violence. Manipulation. Everything was on the table when an addict needed a hit. *Everything.*

Larkin blew her off. "Colt can handle a strung-out druggie."

"You're underestimating the threat."

"You're not giving Colt enough credit."

Dani bit back another retort. Arguing with Larkin would get her nowhere. "We're wasting time. I'm leaving." She strode to the door without looking back. If no one wanted to admit Colt could be in trouble, fine. She would rescue him all by herself.

She reached for the door handle when Larkin called out.

"Hold on. I'm coming." His feet thudded on the laminate floor as he loped to catch up with Dani. "I can't let you get yourself killed on some wild goose chase. Colt would never forgive me."

Dani tugged open the apartment door. "What if everything I've said is true and Colt's really in trouble?"

He smiled. "Then I'll owe you an apology."

"I won't hold my breath." Dani ducked out the open door and Larkin followed.

They hit the street side-by-side and Larkin's easygoing nature morphed into army awareness. Gone were the lazy, plodding steps of inside the apartment. In their place were solid strides and glances in every direction. Dani hustled to keep pace.

She hated to admit she was glad he came along, but it was the truth. She leaned a bit closer as they walked. "Thank you for coming."

Larkin nodded. "Finding Colt won't be easy. He could be anywhere."

Dani left that morning before Colt and Larkin divided up their search. She didn't have a clue where Colt had gone.

She glanced at Larkin. With the corners of his mouth

tipped down in a frown, he looked every bit the disgruntled soldier. At twice her age, he must have seen his fair share of missions gone bad. Dani hoped this time he was right and Colt was delayed, but safe. An I-told-you-so chorus would be music to her ears if Colt was okay.

Larkin slowed as he approached the corner and held out his arm for Dani to stop. After he cleared the cross street, she joined him. "Do you know his route?"

He nodded. "More or less."

"Where should we start?"

"At the beginning." Larkin motioned down the street. "The 600 block."

Together, the pair of them navigated past broken windows and abandoned cars, pausing every few storefronts to assess and regroup. Dani debated telling Larkin about Skeeter and his demand for payment. Her mother's debts weren't anyone's concern but her own. But if Skeeter caught any of her friends…

Dani shoved the what-ifs aside. If she remembered right, then Skeeter kept to the blocks south of Prairie, almost half a mile behind them. Big Nicky controlled the streets to the north, all the way up to the edges of town where houses and buildings gave way to forest and wildlife.

Would they still respect the pre-EMP order? She didn't know why not. Even after the grid collapse, a drug dealer wouldn't give up his territory. Not willingly. Dani exhaled.

She was safe from Skeeter for now.

They cleared the block and paused at the entrance

to the first building across the street. "We clear as a team. One hallway at a time. I hit the inside of the apartments, you stand watch."

Dani shot Larkin a look. He was boxing her out? "I can search as well as you can."

He shook his head. "We need a lookout. If Colt's in trouble, there must be a fair number of hostiles. One strung-out loner wouldn't take that man down."

Larkin had a point. If they charged in without cover, they could end up captured or worse. She conceded. "All right. I'll stand watch."

One floor at a time, they cleared the first building. No sign of Colt, other than the complete absence of anything worthwhile. If he'd been ambushed before reaching the building, there would be something of value left behind. A can of peaches or a bottle of dish soap. *Something*.

They moved onto the second, then the third and the fourth. It was never-ending and hopeless.

Two hours later, Larkin stopped at a fifth-floor landing. The apartment building squatted on the corner of the last block of Colt's search area. He ran a dirt-streaked hand over his face, smearing dust and sweat into makeshift war paint across his cheeks. "We're never going to find him."

Dani leaned back against the faded floral wallpaper and used her sleeve to wipe her forehead. "We can't quit."

"It's worse than a needle in a haystack. It's a SEAL in the city. He's too good, Dani."

"Let's search the building. There's only a floor or two left."

"And after that?"

She turned to Larkin, wishing she could argue, but he was right. Colt could be anywhere. If he'd followed a lead or cleared the block early, he could be halfway to Washington state by now, or back home waiting for them. If they didn't stumble upon him in one of the places down the hall, that would be it. Colt would have to find his own way home.

Dani checked the rifle in her hands for the hundredth time that day and shoved down her disappointment. Colt would be all right. He would have to be. She didn't know what she would do without him. He'd saved her life and showed her what it meant to care.

Nothing would be the same if he disappeared. Dani motioned toward the hall. "Those rooms aren't getting any clearer."

Larkin snorted and took off toward the first door. As his shape blended with the gloom of the hall, a teeming crash shook the entire floor.

Dani brought the rifle up and crouched against the wall as Larkin dove to the ground.

He called out from the dark, "See anything?"

"No!" Dani held her breath, waiting for some other sign. She knew it was Colt. It had to be.

CHAPTER SIX

COLT

672 Bellwether Street
    Eugene, Oregon
    1:00 p.m.

A MAN STEPPED INTO VIEW, BUT THE BARREL OF COLT'S own Sig Sauer captured his attention. It pointed sure and steady from the outstretched arm of the closet girl's father.

Colt dragged his eyes up the length of cold metal and met the gaze of the temporary owner. Same brown eyes as his little girl, same dirt-caked skin. But that's where the similarities ended. The man's cheeks sucked in with every breath and the scraggly beard coating his jaw quivered. His eyes sat in hollow sockets, too strung out to blink.

No sudden movements. No sleight of hand. Colt couldn't risk it. Drug addicts ran the spectrum from ordinary men with good hearts to the ones who did anything to score. Colt guessed this man fell into the latter camp: resourceful and without morals.

He kept his voice even. "Good trick you've got there, using your kid as bait."

The man's chest puffed with twisted pride. "Thought of it myself."

"How about you let me go?"

The gun rocked back and forth. "Why would I do that?"

"You've got my weapon and all of my things. What good am I as a prisoner?"

"Not a chance. You're staying right here."

"What's the point? Now you'll have to feed me and find a place for me to piss. Just save yourself the hassle and cut me loose."

The father stuck his thumb nail in his mouth and chewed on it. The gun shook in the air. "You're not fooling me."

Colt raised an eyebrow. "About what?"

The man motioned at his daughter. "Go get 'em, baby."

She scampered from the bathroom, her mouth stained in a multi-colored rainbow. Moments later, she returned holding up a pair of sneakers and clothes Colt lifted from another apartment a few doors down.

Her dad tilted his head. "You ain't alone, otherwise you wouldn't be stealin' ladies shoes and jeans. There's more of you somewhere. I want to know where."

"I stole those to trade." Colt widened his stance on

the toilet. Twisted his lips into a smirk. "Women will do anything for shoes. If you know what I mean."

"I don't believe you."

Colt leaned back, feigning boredom. "Suit yourself. But in about five minutes you're gonna regret keeping me here."

"Why?"

"Because I've got to take a shit the size of Mount Everest and I don't think you want me doing it all over your bathroom floor."

"You're sitting on the toilet, asshole. Use it."

Colt tugged on his hands. "I can't. You taped the lid shut."

The druggie swore and rubbed at his face with his free hand. The gun barrel wobbled all over the place. If Colt only had a bit of leverage, he could take the man out with a well-placed kick. But it wouldn't get him anything but a hard time.

He needed out of the damn duct tape. Colt squirmed around on the seat and screwed up his face like he couldn't hold it.

"Eeww, Daddy, what's that smell?" The little girl pinched her nose and stuck out her tongue.

"Sorry, man. Like I said, I gotta go."

The girl's father stared at Colt. It was like watching a film in slow motion. All the options paraded through his head one after the other and washed across his face plain as day. Shoot him? No. He had a kid to think about. Leave him there and let him take a dump all over the place? No. He didn't want to clean up the mess. Let him go? Not a chance.

The guy stood there, confused and unsure while Colt squirmed. "Come on, man. If I let loose in these pants, you'll never get the stink out."

"Fine." The girl's father turned to his daughter. "Dump those clothes and go get some scissors. Quick."

She ran out of the room while her father paced back and forth. He ran a hand through his hair every few steps as he waved the gun about. "You try anything and I'll put a bullet in your head, you understand?"

Colt nodded.

The little girl came back and her father pointed at Colt's hands. "Cut one of his hands loose."

He pointed at Colt. "I meant what I said. Not a move.'

Colt inhaled and braced himself for action. He counted on the man's reflexes being too slow. The little girl stepped up to him and bit her lip as she opened the scissors. They were so big, she had to hold one side with each hand.

She opened the blades. Rust pocked the surface. Colt tensed. "You know how to use those things, right?"

"Course she does. Now shut up and let her work." The man nodded at the girl. "Go on, baby. It's all right."

The girl nodded and turned back to the task. Colt twisted to the side to give her the best angle. Were his shots up to date? Dying of some nasty infection after surviving bullet wounds and a three-story fall would be ironic at best.

She stuck the scissors through the gap in Colt's arms and forced them shut. Even from Colt's poor angle, he could see they would never open. The tape stuck to the metal and held fast. The little girl tugged and pulled, but it was no use.

"Daddy, they're stuck. I can't do it." She sagged and looked up at him.

The man didn't know what to do. He shook his head back and forth, opened his mouth and closed it again, glanced all around the bathroom.

Colt spoke up. "You got a knife? A sharp one will probably cut through it."

The drug addict mumbled curses beneath his breath and shoved the gun in his waistband. He stepped forward and yanked on the scissors. It took him three tries and some serious effort, but he pulled them free. He turned to his daughter. "You watch him honey, and if he does anything, you holler. All right?"

The girl nodded and her father left the room.

Colt couldn't wait there forever. Every minute this circus kept up, his chances of escape dwindled. The man would either get sick of him or do something stupid and someone would die. Colt hoped it wouldn't be the little girl.

"How about you go take a nap, huh, sweetie? I bet you're tired after all that candy."

She rose up on one foot, balancing like a ballerina. "I'm not tired. I could stay up all day and all night, just like Daddy."

"If you dig through my bag, you'll find a pack of gum in the bottom. You can have it."

She twirled around on her toes with her arms up in the air. "I don't like gum. Too chewy."

Colt exhaled. He didn't want the kid there when he

took on her father. "There might be some clothes. Something pretty for you."

The girl paused halfway through another turn. "Like a necklace or a tiara?"

Colt plastered on a smile. "You never know unless you find out."

Her father stepped back into the room holding a giant bread knife with a foot-long blade. The little girl squeezed under his arm and scampered away. He watched her go and shook his head. "Kids. They can't never stay in one place."

"She seemed to like the closet just fine."

The man pinned Colt with a look. "Keep talkin' like that and I'll leave you here, shit or no shit."

Colt managed another nod and turned his back on the man.

The knife blade rubbed against his forearm as the man slipped it between Colt's hands. He sawed it back and forth against the tape. Little by little the tension in Colt's arms eased. He worked on keeping his body relaxed and easy. Too much tension and the man might notice.

The first section of tape gave way. He could move his shoulders. A minute later, the man hacked through the next section and Colt's wrists separated, but he was still taped to the toilet.

Colt pointed with his head at the toilet seat. "You'll have to cut the tape on the seat, too."

The man shot him a look. "I ain't stupid. Hold on." He crouched down in an awkward sideways stance with the gun digging into his ribs. As he worked on the tape, Colt ran through the options. Only one came to mind.

He inhaled. Focused his mind. Waited. Almost there…

The second the tape connecting his right hand to the toilet separated Colt dove for the gun. He wrapped his fingers around the butt and yanked it free as the man staggered back.

With a shout, the man swung the knife. Colt ducked and it went wide. Spinning around, Colt grabbed the toilet seat in his left hand and yanked with all his might. It ripped from the toilet.

Colt fell back from the force, landing hard inside the tub. His legs stuck up in the air and he couldn't get leverage. The drug addict lunged for him again with the knife. Colt cocked the gun, aimed, and pulled the trigger.

It clicked.

Shit.

The man laughed and lunged for him again. "You think I'd wave a loaded gun around with a kid in here?" he jabbed at Colt with the knife. It sliced his shirt and nicked his side.

He grunted and heaved himself out of the tub with all his strength. He collided with the man and propelled him back. The man's hip hit the side of the sink and the knife clattered to the floor.

Colt whipped the gun around in his grip and used it like a club. Swinging high and fast, he slammed the butt into the side of the man's head and he went down, crumpling into the sink before sliding onto the floor.

A scream rose up from the doorway. The little girl stood there, wearing one of the shirts Colt picked out for Dani. It reached her knees.

He stepped over her father and brushed past her. He couldn't save them all.

CHAPTER SEVEN

DANI

672 BELLWETHER STREET
Eugene, Oregon
2:00 p.m.

THE DOOR TO AN APARTMENT CRASHED OPEN AND DANI brought up the rifle. She squinted into the dark and took aim as a shape barreled into the hall. Her finger twitched on the trigger.

"It's all right, Dani!" Larkin bellowed. "It's Colt!"

She eased off the trigger and lowered the rifle as Colt and Larkin approached.

Colt reached for her and brought her to his chest for a quick hug. "We need to move, now."

She pulled back and looked at him. Blood matted half of his hair and duct tape hung in twisted strips around his wrists. "Are you all right?"

He nodded. "I'll fill you in later. Right now we need to hurry."

The three of them rushed down the stairs and into the dilapidated lobby without another word. Larkin peered out the dirty glass. "Do we need to hole up somewhere or head straight back?"

"Let's loop around to the south and come up from the other direction."

"Copy that." Larkin pushed open the door and glanced around. "It's clear." He headed out with Colt and Dani on his heels.

They kept to the shadows, ducking into doorways and pausing in alleys as they navigated toward the south. Dani thought about Skeeter. She couldn't be seen on the street. Not with Colt and Larkin.

On the edge of his territory, she grabbed Colt by the arm. "There's a dealer down here looking for my mom. We're almost in his 'hood. If he spots me, it'll be bad."

Colt pulled her into a doorway hidden from the street and whistled for Larkin. A moment later, he joined them.

"How bad?"

Dani exhaled. "He said my mom owes him two hundred. Owes a bunch of other dealers, too. Next time he sees me, he wants his money."

"They're still using money?"

"Skeeter, is I guess. Maybe all the dealers. Most people around here don't have checking accounts. That's why there's so many check-cashing places and Western Unions. People don't use credit cards or ATMs in this neighborhood."

"Larkin, you have any cash?"

He shook his head. "Not a dollar."

"I don't, either." Colt frowned. "Will Skeeter leave his territory?"

"No. Never. Big Nicky works up here. Skeeter knows not to cross him."

"All right. Let's skirt the edge. If we can make it home without being followed or getting into any more trouble, we can decide what to do about Skeeter later."

Colt filled her and Larkin in about his kidnapping and Dani fought to keep her emotions in check. She knew Colt had been in trouble. She shot Larkin a glance. He shrugged.

"What's the chance the guy will come after us?"

"Probably low. But we should go back to the apartment where we know it's secure."

Dani nodded and let Larkin once again take the lead. This time she kept pace, pointing out the edges of Skeeter's territory and ensuring they stayed on the right side. An hour later, they arrived at the apartment building without incident.

They eased around the back and slipped in the rear door. Thanks to their work a few days before, the front appeared abandoned, but it was actually the most secure entrance on the block. Two by fours and plywood blocked any attempt at breaking in, combined with heaps of trash behind them. Even if an enterprising person worked their way inside, they would have to contend with broken glass and rats before they made it to the back.

Dani took the stairs two at a time and beat both men

to the top. She opened the apartment door and waited. Her heart thudded against her chest in exertion and relief. As soon as Colt and Larkin slipped in, she shut and locked it and leaned against the wall. *Colt is safe.* She said the three words over and over again in her head until she believed them to be true.

Colt reached out and gave her arm a squeeze. "I'm calling a meeting."

Dani nodded as he walked away, not trusting her voice to stay even. She closed her eyes and thought about how dangerous their current situation had become. They couldn't stay in Eugene. It wasn't worth the odds.

After her heart slowed, Dani peeled herself off the wall and took a seat in the living room. Everyone else was already there. Harvey, Gloria, and their grandson Will. Melody and her brother Doug. Colt and Larkin. Even little Lottie, the yorkie, sat on Melody's lap, licking a front paw.

Colt cleared his throat. "As you all know, we've been scraping by so far outside of the militia's control. But things are deteriorating rapidly. I don't believe staying here any longer is sustainable or wise. I called this meeting to propose a new course of action."

He paused and glanced around the room. "It's time to leave Eugene."

At first, no one spoke. Melody glanced at Gloria. Harvey glanced down at his grandson. Larkin leaned back in his chair and closed his eyes. It was like Colt had told them the Ducks wouldn't win the division or there was no such thing as Santa.

Dani didn't understand it. She'd been saying they should leave Eugene for days. Even before the Wilkinses and Harpers lost their houses in the fire. Even before she was shot and left for dead.

They couldn't stay in a town where a madman wanted to kill them and make a show of it. She shifted on her chair and waited.

At last, Harvey broke the silence. "Where do you propose we go?"

"South. The farther south we go, the better the winter weather. I know it's only April, but we need to think about freezing temperatures and snowfall."

"I have friends in Reno." Melody smiled at everyone as she tucked her legs beneath her. "We could head there."

Colt thought it over. "Reno's too big. But Lake Tahoe is an option. It should have fish and plenty of cabins."

Harvey leaned back and shook his head. "They're what? Five hundred miles from here? I'll die of old age before we get there."

"Not necessarily." Larkin opened his eyes. "We have vehicles, don't forget that."

Colt nodded. "The electric car is dead, but the Corolla we found in the garage has half a tank. The Humvee's range isn't great, but somewhere will have diesel to siphon." He glanced around at the seven other people in the room. "It'll be a tight squeeze, but we can make do."

"What about food? Clothes? Shelter while we're on the road?" Doug scooted forward on the love seat, and braced his elbows on his knees. "We've got a good thing going here. The place is secure. It's warm. We've been capturing rainwater and scavenging for food. I say we stay."

Dani spoke up. "There's too many bad people still hanging out. Drug dealers my mom used to know, addicts looking for a fix. It's too dangerous."

"We've been doing fine."

She hesitated, but Colt gave her the go-ahead. "One of them stopped me today. Said my mom owes him money. If I don't pay him, he's going to come looking."

"Your mother's debts don't have anything to do with us."

"Doug!" Melody admonished her brother, but he ignored her.

"It's true. We shouldn't have to leave because Dani's got a problem with some thug."

Dani crossed her arms and focused on the floor.

"It's not just her." Colt shifted in his seat. "I was ambushed today while on a run." He turned and showed off the blood on his head. "Lucky for me the guy was too weak to kill me. But it took some serious work to get away. He's still out there. Looking for me."

"Great." Doug rolled his eyes. "Where have I heard this before?"

"You could always stay behind." Larkin stayed in a slouch, but the edge in his voice made his meaning clear.

Gloria held up her hands. "Let's not fight. Doug, I hear you on wanting everyone to stay. Colt and Dani, I understand why you want to leave. Melody, what do you think?"

The younger woman glanced at her brother before responding. "I think we should go."

Doug made a noise, but she ignored it.

"Jarvis will be looking for us. At some point, he'll come this way. We need to be far away from Eugene when that happens. I don't think we would survive another attack." She reached for her brother's arm. "I don't want to go through that again, Doug."

Doug's snotty look faded, and he scooted closer to his sister on the couch. He reached out and squeezed her knee. "Are you sure?"

"Very."

He exhaled with a nod. "All right. Then I guess I'm in."

Colt turned to Harvey. "What do you say?"

"I don't like it, but I know you're right. Leaving is the only option."

"Then it's settled. We can get everything assembled and packed today and hit the road first thing tomorrow morning."

Dani stayed in her seat while everyone else stood up and stretched before wandering off to their respective rooms. She knew they had to leave, but it still filled her with dread. Driving all the way to some lake on the border of California?

Without gear or supplies or even warm coats, how would they make it across two states? She chewed on her lip as she thought about all the things that could go wrong. From Jarvis finding them as they headed out, to the Humvee breaking down in the middle of nowhere, to not finding a place to stay once they made it.

Leaving Eugene was the right call, but could they really make it that far? She glanced up to find Colt watching her from the kitchen. He'd stacked up all the bottles of water on the counter and was starting in on the little food they hadn't yet eaten.

She managed a smile. Maybe she was overreacting. Maybe it wouldn't be so hard.

DAY THIRTY-ONE

CHAPTER EIGHT

MELODY

672 Bellwether Street
   Eugene, Oregon
   7:00 a.m.

Steady raindrops hummed in the background while Melody balanced two bottles of water on her hip. Unable to sleep, she'd crawled out of bed at five and stood on the edge of the balcony, staring out over the town she'd called home her entire life.

The clouds hid the stars and through the rain she couldn't see a single light. The University sat dark this chilly, wet morning. She glanced down at the water she cradled like an infant and forced a dry swallow. Kids had always been on the horizon; she wanted a family someday.

Now they seemed like a distant dream, almost as ethereal as electricity. Never would she tickle chubby little marshmallow feet or dance barefoot in the grass with a little girl that had her eyes. At twenty-seven, Melody felt for the first time like she'd wasted her life.

Sure, she'd become a veterinary technician and helped pet dogs and cats and even a pig or two when they came to the vet. But she'd put so many things on hold. Travel. A boyfriend. Family.

She hadn't even read a good book in months. Now there wouldn't be any new books or bookstores to find them in. No coffee shops to while away the morning, no museums in which she could lose an afternoon.

The buildings were all still standing, but for how long? How long would any of it last without the government propping them up? When they hadn't heard from the mayor or the governor or the president, how could they expect to ever go back to normal?

A bottle slipped and she clutched it tighter. The closest she would ever get to a baby in her arms.

"Need a hand?"

Melody spun around. Larkin stood a few feet away, freshly shaven and smiling. A month ago she wouldn't have given him a second glance. A soldier? No way. But now…

He'd risked his own life to save hers and turned his back on the military he'd loved. She smiled back. "There's four more on the counter. I couldn't carry them."

Larkin nodded and turned away. She'd never noticed before how his eyes caught the light and sparkled. Melody followed him into the kitchen and waited as he picked up the bottles. One slipped from his grip and he ended up carting them all in front of him like a bushel of apples.

"I don't know how you women balance anything on a hip."

"Instinct, I guess."

He stilled. "Did you have any—"

"Kids?" Melody shook her head. "No. I'd wanted to, but…"

"You thought you had more time."

She nodded.

"Sounds familiar." Larkin walked to the door and bent to turn the handle. He bobbled the armload and almost dropped all the water, but managed to hang on. "I told myself I didn't need to settle down until forty. What I wouldn't give now for a plot of land and a white picket fence."

Melody eased through the open door and followed Larkin down the hall. "You're serious?"

He nodded. "Me, a wife, couple of kids, and some land? We could make that work for years and never need to see another living soul." He paused at the landing. "It's too late for that, I'm afraid."

Melody fell silent as she descended the stairs, only resuming the conversation when she reached the lobby. "You really think it's over?"

"What?"

"A normal life."

Larkin paused at the door to the garage. "This *is* normal. Now, anyway." He pushed the door to the garage open with his back. Colt caught it on the other side.

"How's everything upstairs?"

"Everyone else is still asleep."

Colt nodded. "We need to canvas the area for some gas. A few containers if we can find them, too."

"How much fuel does the sedan have?"

"Not enough. Maybe two hundred miles. The Humvee is worse."

Melody let Colt take the bottles from her arms. "How are we going to get to Lake Tahoe with so little?"

"We have to siphon it. Larkin and I are about to go scouting. Hopefully we'll get lucky and find some diesel, too."

"But first things first." Larkin set his bottles in the back of the vehicle and turned around. "We eat some breakfast."

Melody laughed and shook her head. "Men. All you ever think about is food."

Larkin grinned and strode past her. "Not all the time, Ms. Harper."

She watched him walk away until the door to the building shut behind him.

"You stare too long, you might go blind."

Melody spun around. "I wasn't staring."

"And I'm not telling." Colt wiped his hands on a rag and nodded at the door. "He's a good man, Melody. You could do worse."

"I—" She hesitated, unsure what to say. After a moment, she settled on the truth. "There's nothing going on between us."

"Do you want there to be?"

"I don't know." Melody pushed her hair behind her ear. "Would it bother you?"

Colt tilted his head. "Me? Don't think I have any say in the matter."

She ran her tongue over her lower lip. She didn't know why his opinion mattered, but it did. "So that's a no?"

"It wouldn't bother me."

"Good." She stood there, not sure what else to say. She shifted her weight back and forth on her feet, all of a sudden awkward and shy.

Colt's expression didn't change. "You should probably get going."

Melody nodded and turned around. She could feel his eyes on her all the way inside.

After climbing the five flights of stairs, she paused at the door to the apartment. Maybe a family wasn't impossible now. She thought about Larkin's comment about a house with some land and a white picket fence. If the right man came along and they could find a place to settle down…

The door to the apartment opened and her brother and Harvey spilled out, both carrying bags and rifles. They stopped when they saw her.

"You okay, Mel?"

She forced a smile. "Just tired."

"You can probably sleep on the drive."

She nodded at her brother as he walked past her. Whatever the future held, they needed to leave Eugene to make it happen. It was time they got on with it.

An hour later, Melody was back downstairs, standing

outside the two cars along with everyone else. Lottie sat in the crook of her arm, quiet and still.

Colt raised a hand for quiet. "Larkin and I have siphoned all the gas from nearby cars we could manage. It's given us a mostly full tank in the Corolla."

"As soon as we find a vehicle running on diesel, we'll do the same with the Humvee." Larkin pulled out a piece of paper with a hand-drawn map. "Thanks to Harvey's handiwork we have a rough idea of where we're going."

He pointed at a star. "This is where we are." He traced a line from the star to a meandering blue strip halfway across the page. "This is the Willamette River. The main bridges across are three highways. The 569, the 105, and the 5. The lower two will be guarded by Jarvis's troops for sure."

Doug spoke up. "So how do we get across?"

"There's a small bridge here, just south of the 569. Harvey thinks it's our best shot."

"It's a lot closer to the University than the 569." Doug shook his head. "I say we try the highway first."

"We're in a stolen Humvee. If the militia has any lookouts, they'll spot us and put it together. We'll be too exposed on the highway."

Melody stared at the map while the men argued about the best way to cross the river. At last, she spoke up. "I don't think we should cross the river at all. Let's head west, away from Eugene and Springfield. We can get away from Jarvis faster and easier that way, then loop around and head southeast."

"That would add hundreds of miles to the journey."

Harvey walked up to the map and pointed. "We need to take 58 through the national forest. If we head west, there's no good way to get there."

"What are you talking about? We can take I-5 straight south. It'll save hours."

Colt shook his head. "Not gonna happen. I-5 is probably a parking lot by now. Think about all the people that ran out of gas trying to get somewhere. It'll be full of looters and thieves. We need to stay on the back roads. Go unnoticed."

Melody frowned. "You're sure there isn't another way?"

"Not that we know of without a map."

"I lost all my maps in the fire." Harvey kicked at the dirt as he remembered. "I can get us to 58 without one, but I don't know much more than that."

"Then it's settled." Larkin handed Colt the hand-drawn map. "We head to the smaller bridge first. If it's out, we regroup, head up to the 569."

Melody still didn't like the idea. Who knew what waited on the other side of the river?

She ran a hand over Lottie's fur. The little dog would have to sit on her lap the entire drive to Lake Tahoe if they didn't find a carrier to use. It wasn't the bet mode of travel, but Melody wouldn't give up Lottie for the world. The dog would just have to adjust. Like they all did.

She hoisted the last of the supplies into the back of the car and everyone divided up into the vehicles. Colt took the sedan with the Wilkinses and Larkin motioned for Melody to join him, Doug, and Dani in the Humvee. Colt pulled out of the parking spot and Larkin followed.

Melody watched out the window while they turned onto the road. The rain pelted the car in a million little goodbyes. She was leaving her hometown behind for good.

CHAPTER NINE

COLT

He spotted the wreckage a few seconds before anyone else. Colt slowed the car. The windshield wipers sloshed the rain, but did nothing to hide the obvious.

"Jarvis blew all the bridges."

Colt nodded in Harvey's direction. "That's why no one from Springfield is coming to Eugene. They can't get through."

After finding the small bridge blown to bits, with not even the foundation left as evidence, Colt's optimism had faded. He backtracked to Highway 569, expecting the worst. Finding the highway's bridge shorn in two turned any thoughts of an easy passage out of Eugene to dust. They would either have to drive all the way around like Melody suggested in the first place, or find another way across.

Colt sat in the car, listening to the raindrops and windshield wipers, lost in his own frustrated thoughts. No one said a word. Not even teenaged Will in the backseat.

Ever since the ambush and the fires, the boy had been quiet. Docile, even. Colt couldn't tell if it was a good sign. The kid had lived a pretty sheltered life before the power went out. Did the last week of gunshots and fires and ambushes kill Will's spirit or awaken something new?

Colt turned to Harvey at last. "Is there another way across?"

"Not a man-made one." Harvey caught his wife's attention. "Gloria, do you remember that cut-through we used to use up by the Harralson farm?"

"That old thing? No one's used it for years. And we're in a car. We would never make it."

Harvey reached for the map and pointed to a curve in the river. "If we follow the frontage road for about a mile, there used to be a family farm tucked in the bend. In the low-rain months, we crossed the river on four-wheelers. There was a sand bar on this side and the river broke into smaller tributaries we could jump."

Colt peered out at the rain. It had been coming down thick for hours and had rained on and off for the last few days. Good for catching rain water, bad for crossing a river. "What's the chance it's passable now?"

"I don't even know if it's still there." Harvey handed the map back to Colt. "But it's worth a shot, isn't it?"

After a moment, Colt nodded. "Can't hurt to look." He rolled down the car window, stuck his hand out, and whirled it in the air, signaling a turn-around to Larkin.

They rolled in their two-vehicle caravan down the frontage road, Colt on the lookout for a bend in the river or any place low enough to cross. Harvey thumped the window on his side of the car. "This is it."

Colt parked and climbed out. What used to be a sand bar was now a shallow widening of the river. Water lapped at the bank, spreading all the way to the other side. It appeared passable in the shallows, but the middle ran swift and deep. The car would never make it.

He swiped the rain out of his eyes as Larkin came to stand beside him. "This is the best shot, isn't it?"

"Afraid so. Can the Humvee make it?"

"It's got a deep water kit. Assuming there's not a chasm ten feet deep, yeah. We can get across." Larkin leaned back to look at the little car. "But that thing doesn't stand a chance."

Colt rubbed the beard on his chin. "It's already mid-morning. If we circle back around town to the west, we'll be hours from anywhere when the sun sets."

"We'll run out of diesel long before then." Larkin glanced up to the sky, calculating in his head. "It's lower than I thought. We've got a hundred miles if we're lucky. Eighty is more likely."

Shit. That would barely get them out of Eugene.

"Even if we had enough diesel, the Humvee will never fit all of us and the gear."

Colt glanced at the vehicle. It was an old army Humvee, designed to seat four with room for gear in the back. "We can make it work for a few miles until we find another car."

Larkin squinted at Colt. "That blow to the head must have scrambled your brains. Even if the girls sit on the floor, what do we do with all the gear?"

Colt snorted out a laugh. "I'm not addled, just desperate." He wiped his mouth and leaned closer. "We can't be on the road with everyone into the night. We'll be sitting ducks. Anyone with half a brain and scruples to match would ambush us."

Larkin turned his attention back to the river. "It'll be a wet crossing, assuming we make it."

Colt figured as much. "Don't tell them. It'll only make them more resistant. We've got to find a place to hole up that's dry and has a good, defensible perimeter. We can do that if we head into Springfield. It'll have gas and diesel."

"And another car."

Colt nodded. "The other way is just forest."

Larkin wiped the rain from his eyes and stared out at the river. "The lowest point is up there, where it bends. We'll be halfway into the river before the water comes in. Even if we get across, it won't be easy."

"It never is." Colt clapped him on the back and headed to the car to break the news.

* * *

"This is never going to work." Gloria sat in the back with Lottie on her lap and her grandson at her feet. Harvey sat on the other side with Doug wedged into the footwell and Colt crouched on the corrugated divider in the middle. Not the most comfortable Humvee ride, that was for damn sure.

Melody shifted in the front where she shared a seat with Dani. "I can't feel my feet."

Dani laughed. "I can't see my feet."

Colt shook his head. "If we can get across this river, then we'll be able to find another car."

Larkin eased the Humvee into the water. It bounced and slipped on the sand and Larkin slowed even more. The water lapped at the hood and the doors. The river was swallowing them whole.

"Hold your valuables up, everybody." Larkin clipped each word with tension. "It's deeper than I thought."

"What's that mean?" Dani twisted around as the Humvee plunged ahead into the river. "Colt?"

He opened his mouth, but Melody's scream filled the silence. "My feet! They're getting wet!"

Will jumped up from the floor and clambered up on top of his grandmother's lap. "Water's coming in. Everywhere!"

Doug scrambled to half-stand, practically on top of Harvey. Lottie let out a frantic bark and jumped at Colt, clawing her way up onto the divider. Water sloshed against the floorboards, first a little puddle, then more and more, until it threatened to spill over laps and bags.

Colt thrust his backpack up in the air. Others followed suit. They looked like a bad sitcom come to life. Only there wouldn't be a soundstage and a wardrobe trailer when they reached the other side. The vehicle lurched into a dip in the river bed and the water crested over Gloria's knees.

Melody shrieked.

"It's okay, everyone. I know what I'm doing." Larkin steered the Humvee through the water, over and down rocks hidden beneath the surface of the water. "We could drive this thing deeper than I am tall and the engine would keep running."

"That doesn't make me feel any better!" Melody clutched the door while Dani held onto the seat back.

Most of the color had drained from Gloria's face as she clutched her grandson to her chest. Doug gripped the back of Larkin's seat with a grimace. Even Harvey had grown pensive and still.

The river splashed over the hood and Larkin slowed. "It's going to get a little dicey now. Hang on."

He gripped the steering wheel with both hands and Colt took a deep breath. So far, Larkin proved himself to be an excellent driver, although Colt knew at this point in his career he probably never sat behind the wheel. Majors didn't drive anymore.

The front of the Humvee disappeared beneath the water and a torrent rushed inside.

"We're going to drown in this stupid tin can!"

Melody's shout pierced through the grinding of the gears and the rain, but Larkin grinned. He leaned toward the passenger seat. "Steel and aluminum, to be accurate. Not tin."

She cursed at him and he eased down on the accelerator. The Humvee lurched and for the first time since entering the river, began its ascent. The vehicle gained momentum, rumbling up and over a chunk of rocky river bottom.

Colt exhaled. They might just make it.

Everyone fell silent. Harvey closed his eyes as he clutched the door. Gloria held onto her grandson like he would drag her to safety. Even Melody stopped mumbling. The Humvee rocked and skidded up the muddy bank, but Larkin did it. Water poured out of the floorboards and the tires crunched over the sandy shore of the river.

The tires dug into the road's shoulder and Larkin eased it up onto the asphalt before shifting to park. They had crossed the river.

Melody reached out the second he let go of the steering wheel and swatted Larkin on the arm. "That's for making fun of me." She hit him harder. "That's for driving straight into that dip in the river." She curled her hand in a fist and tried to punch him, but he caught her swing with his open palm.

"What's that one for?"

"Getting my shoes all wet, you jerk."

Larkin let her hand go and laughed so hard it shook the back seat. "What's a little river crossing if there's not an element of surprise." He turned to Colt. "Am I right?"

Colt shook his head and tried to contain his own laughter. "Just find us another car, will you?"

"Yes, sir." Larkin winked before turning his attention back to the road.

CHAPTER TEN

DANI

Streets of Springfield, Oregon
11:00 a.m.

Larkin drove the Humvee through the streets of Springfield just above a crawl. The town reminded Dani of pictures of war zones she'd seen in history class. Blown-apart buildings reduced to rubble, trash in the streets, a car turned black from soot.

Thirty days without power and the residents of Springfield had torn the town apart. For all that she hated Colonel Jarvis and what he did to her and her grandmother, his men kept Eugene orderly. She frowned as she stared out the tinted windows. They passed a row of shops and Larkin slowed to get a better look.

A restaurant with overturned tables and a burned and blackened kitchen. A grocery store with nothing left but broken glass and destroyed shelves. A massive freezer unit sat on its side, door hanging open and empty. It was all so senseless.

Dani pulled her sweatshirt closer around her body and tucked her hands inside her sleeves. No one inside the Humvee said a word. Not even Will. They all stared, open-mouthed and confused, at the remains of the town.

Melody shifted on the seat they shared and Dani risked a glance in the woman's direction. No color in her cheeks, no fire in her eyes. Nothing but shock and dismay. Just like Dani.

Only Colt and Larkin didn't seem fazed. Maybe they had seen it all before in another country halfway around the world. Dani turned back to the window and caught the glimpse of a body sprawled out on the sidewalk, dead and decomposing.

Every block held more of the same, but the farther they drove, the more life Dani spotted. A face peering out from a gaping window. A flash of light in an apartment three stories off the ground. A blur of movement in a shop cordoned off with steel security bars.

The town wasn't empty. Not by a long shot. She twisted around. "I don't have a good feeling about this."

Colt kept his eyes on the road. "We don't have a choice. We need another car and fuel. A city is the best place to find both."

The Humvee slowed and Dani shifted her gaze. A massive dumpster blocked three quarters of the street. Larkin straightened up in the driver's seat. "I'll need to jump the curb. Hold on."

He eased the Humvee up onto the sidewalk and eased toward the dumpster.

Melody shouted, "Watch out!"

A woman jumped in front of the vehicle and Larkin slammed on the brakes. Everyone flew forward in their seats. Dani hit the dash and Melody fell on top of her. The Humvee swayed with the aftershocks.

"Help me! You've got to help me!" The woman rushed forward, arms thrust up in the air as she came around to Larkin's window. Her palms landed smack on the glass. "Please! I need to get out of here!"

Larkin eased the Humvee forward a foot and the woman scrabbled at the door.

"Stop! You'll run her over!" Melody twisted around and Dani almost lost purchase on the seat. "She needs help!"

"Not ours." Larkin eased the vehicle forward another foot, but the woman kept hanging on.

"I've got a daughter. She's sick and needs medicine. Please!"

Melody spun around to the back. "We can't ignore her."

"Yes we can. And we will." Colt kept his voice even, but Dani could hear the tension in it. He was worried.

She glanced out the window and her stomach hit the floor. "More are coming from the right. I count four from the storefront on the corner." Dani squinted to get a better view. "Two men and two women. No weapons that I can see."

Colt leaned forward. "Speed it up, Larkin. We don't need a mob."

Larkin hit the gas and the woman still scrabbling against the door shrieked as she lost her grip.

"What are you doing? She needs us." Melody turned to Dani. "Open the door, I want to get out."

Dani's eyes went wide. "Are you crazy? You're going to get us all killed."

"No, I'm not. That woman needs help. We can do something."

"It's called driving." Dani pointed out the window. "Look around you, Melody. These people aren't coming out of the ashes because they want to invite us home for a glass of iced tea and a piece of pie. They want to take advantage."

"You don't know that."

"Yes, I do."

Colt chimed in. "Dani's right. We're a giant moving target in this thing. People see it and they think we're military come to save them. When they find out we're not, they'll be furious. It won't end well for anyone."

Melody shook her head. "I don't believe you. It's only been a month. Good people wouldn't turn bad in a month." She reached past Dani for the door, but Dani grabbed her by the shoulders.

She pinned her to the seat back. "You're not listening. We stop this car and it's over. A mob will be on us before you can get five words out. You think Jarvis was bad? He'll seem like a piece of cake compared to a horde of angry, starving people."

Melody scrunched up her face. "How would you know?"

"Have you ever been so hungry you stole? Have you

ever been consumed by the need for food so bad, you'd do anything, say anything, to get it?"

Melody stilled.

Dani almost spat. "I have. And it's a real bitch. So don't you sit there on your high horse and tell me to open the door. I know what those people are going through. Only they have it worse."

Harvey spoke up from the back. "As much as it hurts, Melody, Danielle is right. We can't stop here. It's too dangerous. We have to think about our own survival. We have to put the needs of the people inside this vehicle first."

Doug added his own voice to the mix. "I don't like it either, Mel, but Harvey's right. We have to think about all of us right now."

Melody's brows dipped low as she focused on her brother. "It's not right."

"Nothing is going to be right in this town again." Larkin accelerated down a clear section of the street and left the gaggle of people behind. He turned south and headed toward state road 58 and Lake Tahoe. "If we don't find a place to hole up for the night and some damn fuel for this beast of a vehicle, we won't be any better off. Hell, we'll be worse."

Dani let Melody go and she sagged against the seat. It had to be hard for a woman like her, who had taken food and shelter and basic necessities for granted, to transition to this new way of life. For once Dani was thankful she'd had a terrible time of it. At least she didn't mind the hunger pains and the dirty hair.

Colt spoke up from the back. "Everyone keep your

eyes out for other people on the streets and a place that could work to make camp. It needs to be secure and unobtrusive."

They drove around Springfield for what seemed like hours, finding nothing but more strangers desperate for hope they couldn't deliver. No diesel. No shelter. No food.

Larkin kept glancing down at the dash every minute or so. They were going to run out of fuel. Dani chewed on her lip and stared out at the town. After driving through most of downtown, they transitioned into a residential area where the houses were more or less intact.

"Maybe we could find an empty house and use it."

"No fuel in a house." Larkin shifted up front. "Pretty soon no fuel in this Humvee, either."

Colt leaned forward. "Let's find a restaurant. Fast food or quick service."

"I hate to break it to you, but the drive-thru won't be open."

Colt cracked a smile. "That's what I'm hoping for." He made eye contact with Dani and something in the way he looked at her made her pause. He was optimistic.

It didn't make sense. She turned to look out the window and watch. A few miles down the road she tapped on the glass. "There's a Chili's there on the corner." She couldn't keep the excitement out of her voice. "The windows are boarded up. I don't see a car."

Larkin turned the corner and eased the Humvee over toward the restaurant. "I always liked their southwestern egg rolls. Weird, but good." He drove around to the service entrance and parked in between a dumpster and the back door. "I hope you've got more than just a craving for comfort food."

Colt handed up a rifle and Larkin took it. "If I'm right, we'll find everything we need. Doug, you stay here as guard. Larkin, Dani, and I will clear the building."

Dani nodded and climbed out into the damp Oregon air.

CHAPTER ELEVEN

DANI

CHILI'S
 Springfield, Oregon
 2:00 p.m.

WHILE LARKIN PICKED THE BACK DOOR, COLT PULLED Dani aside. "We don't know what's on the other side of that door. Those boarded up windows mean either the manager took some precautions or someone's inside and doesn't want to be found."

Dani hoped for option number one. Larkin stood up and Colt stepped back, gun aimed and ready. Dani sucked in a breath. It wasn't any different than the neighborhood searches she'd been doing all week, but she couldn't stop the tremor in her hands.

Larkin turned the handle and pulled the door open. The misty light from outside lit a wedge of linoleum and Colt took the lead. Dani eased in behind him and Larkin followed. The door shut and sealed them inside.

Dani's heart pounded so loud she missed Colt's instruction. Larkin prodded her in the back and she side-stepped down the hall, following blindly as her eyes sucked up the inky dark.

She couldn't see more than a foot in any direction. The end of the rifle blended into the shadows and Colt was more a feeling than a person two steps away.

Colt tapped her on the arm and she jumped. He motioned toward the kitchen, two fingers up and to the right. He wanted her to follow. She nodded and fell in step behind him. Her back grazed the wall as they ducked inside the commercial space.

What she wouldn't give for some fancy military gear. Back at the University, Larkin probably had access to all sorts of crazy stuff like night vision goggles and scopes. Colt stopped a few yards into the kitchen and leaned back against the wall, handgun up and ready. Dani followed suit.

They stood in the darkness, waiting while the frustration built and their eyes adjusted.

After a few minutes, the kitchen work surfaces separated from the dark beyond and Dani could make out enough to navigate. Colt motioned for her to clear the south corner and she took off, ducking behind a long prep surface to investigate the metal shelving beyond.

Everything appeared more or less intact. No turned-over shelves, no empty cans of food thrown about. Vandals hadn't turned it into a trashcan. She worked her way slowly through the gloom, relying on what little light filtered through the gaps in the plywood out front to see. It wasn't much.

A person could be hiding practically anywhere and Dani wouldn't see him until almost too late. But she came up empty. No people in her little corner of the kitchen.

Colt found her waiting where they first separated. "Anything?" His whisper cut the silence like a shout.

"No."

"Good the rest of the kitchen is clear. Bathrooms, too."

Larkin approached a moment later. "Seating area is clear. The place is empty."

Dani exhaled in relief. They found somewhere to hide at least for one night. She didn't know what about the place made Colt want to stop, but she was damp, tired, and ready to relax for a few hours.

Colt flicked on a flashlight and handed it to Dani. "Start searching the kitchen for food and supplies. Start at one end and be systematic. Go through every cabinet, shelf, and cardboard box you can find."

Dani nodded. "What if I find something?"

"If we can use it, put it on the prep table. We can sort it there."

While Colt and Larkin went to gather everyone still inside the Humvee, Dani set to work following his instructions. She started with the prep area, opening doors and drawers one after the other. Nothing but pots and pans and every kind of baking dish ever made. The top racks held serving plates and bowls and saucers, but no food.

She spun around in frustration. Where was it all? Dani had never been inside a kitchen of this scale. Most of her food prep experience came from the nasty counter at her mother's or Gran's tidy little kitchen before she got sick.

They didn't have more than five feet of counter between them. This place was enormous. She thought about what it must be like full with cooks and waiters running around. Where would they keep the food?

Panning the flashlight around the space, she paused on a giant metal door at one end of the kitchen. A fridge and freezer? Dani approached with caution. Everything in there was probably rotten and disgusting, but she had to know.

She wrapped her hand around the handle and brought her arm up to shield her nose from the smell. The door opened with a sucking sound and Dani gagged. Smell wasn't the right word. Putrid, nasty stench from the depths of hell was more like it.

Coughing and hacking, Dani advanced into the room with her sweatshirt tight against her nose. It took all her self-control not to throw up. At one point it had been a fridge. Now black and moldy lumps of produce off-gassed on metal shelves and milk curdled in glass jars.

She grimaced as she stepped farther inside. There had to be something of value in there. Not everything rotted in a month. The room was still cooler than the rest of the place. It couldn't be all bad.

Dani ran the flashlight beam over each shelf, pausing if anything showed promise. A wheel of cheese still encased in wax. She didn't know if it was edible, but it was worth a shot. Three sacks of potatoes on the bottom shelf. A bag of onions. A handful of things that looked like fat, white carrots. A root vegetable? One of those things she'd heard about in books but never seen?

She grabbed the bundle and tossed them along with everything else remotely passable onto an empty cart. It wasn't much, but they could get by for a few days on what she found. As she wheeled the cart out, the rest of the crew piled into the kitchen.

Doug stood in front of the prep counter, rubbing his shoulders and back. The poor guy was too big to cram down around Harvey's feet, and thanks to the river crossing, most of his clothes were still wet.

Melody held Lottie tight to her chest as she looked around the space. Ever since the run-in with the people on the street, she'd been silent. Dani didn't know if she'd been in some sort of denial about how bad things could be, but she hoped Melody would snap out of it.

Harvey and Gloria and Will stood off to one side, huddled in a sad little group.

Everyone looked beat down and out of sorts. Dani pushed the cart up to them all with a smile. "It's not much, but I think we can make some of this work."

Melody wrinkled up her nose. "What's that smell?"

"Rotting vegetables, mostly. I found all this in the fridge. It's as big as a house."

Doug nodded as he rubbed a kink out of his neck. "Commercial kitchens are massive. Have you found the dry goods yet?"

"Not yet."

"I'll look for them."

Dani smiled in thanks and watched as he sauntered off toward the metal shelves on the other side of the kitchen. She was tired and frustrated and rethinking leaving Eugene, but Dani knew it had been the right decision.

They might be cold and wet and hungry, but they were out from under Jarvis's control. He couldn't come after them across the river. It might be the hardest thing any of them had ever done, but hitting the road would turn out to be the best call, she knew it.

Everyone set to work as quickly as possible while they could rely on daylight to mask their flashlights from passersby outside. Gloria and Melody made makeshift sleeping areas in the restaurant using the cushions from the booths and tablecloths from the laundry.

Harvey helped Doug cart dry goods over from the shelving and stage them on the prep table. Larkin found a tarp in the supply closet and used it to cover the Humvee. It wasn't perfect, but it would give them decent cover when night fell.

Colt stood in front of the deep fryer with an empty jug and a scowl. Dani walked up to him. "Don't tell me you want to cook with that stuff. It's got mold growing all over it."

He shook his head. "Not cook. But we need to bottle it somehow."

Dani raised an eyebrow. "What for?"

"You'll see. Look around for some sort of funnel."

Dani couldn't find a funnel, but she came back with

a roll of heavy duty aluminum foil. "I figure we can make one."

Within five minutes, they had fashioned a funnel out of the foil and set it up inside an empty apple juice jug. Colt opened the drain valve on the bottom of the fryer and drained enough oil to fill that jug and five more besides. When they finished, he stood back and smiled. "It might just work."

Dani waited, but he didn't explain and she wasn't going to press him. Whatever he needed nasty used cooking oil for, he could have it.

As the sun began to set outside, everyone collected around three tables Melody had pushed together. With Gloria's help, the pair of women had assembled a veritable feast. Crackers and cheese and still-edible oranges. A massive can of beans and spiced apples. It might as well have been a Christmas goose and hot stuffing like Dani read about last year in school.

They were lucky today.

Gloria held up her glass of water and the table fell silent. "I want to thank Colt and Larkin for all they've done to get us this far. I didn't appreciate how difficult leaving Eugene would be. Without the Humvee or Larkin's driving skills, we would never have crossed the river. Without Colt's quick thinking, we wouldn't be sitting around a table eating and drinking and being merry. So thank you."

Larkin held up his hand. "No thanks necessary." After everyone took a drink, Larkin leaned back in his chair. He glanced around the table and a slow smile spread across his face. "How about we lighten it up a little, huh?" He pointed at Colt. "Favorite song. Go."

Colt broke into a grin. "'Friends in Low Places.'" He pointed to Melody. "Your turn."

She stammered and her cheeks turned red. "You'll laugh."

Larkin drummed the table. "Out with it."

"'Total Eclipse of the Heart.'" She pointed to her brother. "Your turn."

"Red Hot Chili Peppers. 'Under the Bridge.'" Doug pointed at Harvey. "You're up, Wilkins."

"Anything by Bob Seger."

Larkin waggled his finger. "Pick one."

Harvey glanced up at the ceiling. "'Travelin' Man,' I guess. Will, how about you?"

"Anything by Twenty One Pilots." Will beamed, but most everyone around the table drew a blank.

"I don't even know who they are." Larkin shook his head. "Shows how old I'm getting."

"Not as old as some of us." Gloria smiled. "For me, it's 'Coal Miner's Daughter.'"

Dani swallowed as Larkin pointed at her. She didn't know what to say. "I don't really have a favorite song."

"Oh, come on, there has to be one."

She thought about the music her grandmother used to listen to. "Gran always used to listen to musicals. She had an old record player we listened to on Sunday afternoons." Dani smiled. "I always liked the one in *Guys and Dolls*…" She paused as she sang it in her head, trying to remember the title. "'Luck Be A Lady,' I think."

Larkin nodded. "Impressive. One of Frank's best."

"How about you, Larkin? What's your favorite?"

"Me? Oh, I'm a Kenny Rogers guy, through and through. 'The Gambler.' That's my all-time favorite."

Colt leaned back in his chair and looked around. "So we've got a few country fans, a rocker, a cheesy pop lover, and a surprising throwback to the standards." He smiled at Dani and she tried not to blush. Larkin might not have meant to, but thinking of her grandmother made Dani grateful for everyone sitting around the table. She didn't choose this ragtag family, but that's what they had grown to be.

Leaving as a group had been the right call. As everyone finished dinner, Colt excused himself. "I'll take first shift tonight."

Dani spoke up. "I can do it if you want to sleep."

He shook his head. "No. You get some rest. I couldn't sleep if I tried." He picked up a rifle and checked his handgun in his holster before walking toward the front of the restaurant.

"Do you think we'll be safe tonight?" Melody's question voiced the fear percolating in Dani's stomach.

Larkin shrugged. "Only one way to find out."

CHAPTER TWELVE

COLT

CHILI'S
Springfield, Oregon
11:00 p.m.

THE TENUOUS NATURE OF THEIR EXISTENCE HIT COLT full-force as he peered out into the dark. Thanks to the restaurant, they were able to eat and drink and sleep for the night, but it wasn't permanent. The lack of lookout positions drove him crazy.

He'd been all over the damn restaurant, trying to find somewhere to set up for a while. Nowhere worked. A few gaps between the front windows served as a decent vantage point during the day, but were useless at night. The back was all metal and concrete block.

What they needed was height. A little elevation and one or two people could maintain passable security. A one-story restaurant with solid doors and nooks and crannies everywhere wasn't the best option. Not by a long shot. He eased the rear door open and squinted into the night.

Clouds floated across the moon and cast an eerie glow across the parking lot. At least he could see. The door closed with a click behind him and Colt stood still; a dark figure against the beige paint of the wall.

Something about the place was too good to be true. Why wasn't it looted? The location in a mostly residential area? The boarded-up windows? He wasn't sure either counted as sufficient deterrents.

Maybe no one as desperate as the people they'd seen downtown had stumbled across it. They were a long way from the woman crying in the street. He thought about Melody and her inability to process this new reality.

What she didn't understand was that there could be no more charity. Colt's run-in with the father-daughter team of the day before made that clear. Desperation had kicked in for everyone. He pushed off the wall and eased into the parking lot, scanning every few steps in a 360-degree circle.

As a SEAL, preliminary scouting wasn't his specialty. He never patrolled an area, attempting to keep it secure. He went in, did the job, got out. Sticking around wasn't a part of the plan. He hated patrol.

Too many variables. Too many avenues of attack.

Colt walked the perimeter with quiet steps, searching for a place to set up. A tree thirty yards across the lot held promise. So did a spot just behind the restaurant's sign near the road. He could get comfortable, hide behind the unlit sign and watch. He circled the restaurant and paused.

A rustling sound came from the back near the Humvee. He faded into the shadows like a ghost and moved closer.

The tarp.

It shook and shimmied on top of the vehicle. Colt lifted the rifle and held the scope to his eye. *Damn.* Too close to use as a sight. Perfect if he needed to shoot an apple off the Humvee's hood, but terrible to find the source of the noise.

He slung the rifle over his shoulder and pulled out his Sig. Crept another five feet along the building's edge.

"Told you! It's military!"

"*Shh.* They've gotta be inside."

Colt froze. Two unidentified males. He couldn't tell if they were kids or old enough to be dangerous. He hugged the wall and focused on their voices.

"They gotta have guns. We should bust in there. Check it out."

"You got a death wish? They probably already know we're here."

Colt kept the smile to himself. At least one of them had a brain.

"Let's just get inside and check it out."

Damn it. He couldn't let that happen. Colt stepped out of the dark. "You're damn straight I know you're here. Now leave." He leveled the gun at the shape moving about around the vehicle.

"You don't look military to me." The shape shuffled closer and separated into three. *Shit*. Although they couldn't have been older than twenty, what they lacked in age they made up for in size. The one in front outweighed Colt by a good fifty pounds. A big, hulking beast of a kid.

Colt pointed the barrel at his chest. "Guess you've never met a SEAL. I won't ask a third time. Leave."

"Don't sound like you're askin' at all, mister." The smaller of the three stepped forward. "We weren't doin' nuthin'. And this ain't your store anyway. You got no right to ask us to leave."

"That's my vehicle you're poking around." Colt didn't want to shoot them. The gunfire would terrify everyone inside the restaurant and call a ton of unwanted attention. Who knew what the sound of a shootout would bring out of the woodwork.

He made a show of cocking the gun. "You don't want to die over a puffed-up ego. Leave and I won't put a bullet in your head."

The quiet one reached into his pocket. Colt took aim on his chest. As the kid removed his hand, a knife blade caught the moonlight. Colt groaned to himself. *What is it with me and knives lately?* The blade upped the odds of having to shoot. It was still the worst option.

He pointed at the knife with his gun. "You know how to use that thing or just showing off?"

The kid made a swiping motion with the blade. *Guess that's a yes.* Colt widened his stance and unlocked his knees. If only he had Larkin to back him up.

All three young men fanned out, surrounding Colt in a half-circle. He had a choice to make. Use the gun and end this now or do it the hard way.

Shooting them meant at least three bullets, six if he didn't want to take a chance. It would just about run him dry. It would also mean they had to leave as soon as possible. No sleeping in, no calm and orderly breakfast before hitting the road. No chance to wash some of the grime off.

Not that hygiene should come above his own safety, but Colt was sick of being on the defensive. Sick of always being one step behind. After Jarvis, he wanted a break.

The kid with the knife rushed him as he thought it over. A quick jab and Colt parried, dancing back like a boxer. Another stepped forward and swung. Thanks to the kid's size, he telegraphed everything from the angle of the blow to the force of the impact.

Colt dodged again and the kid stumbled as his fist caught nothing but air. Heat rose off the two who missed, their anger reflected in the bunch of their shoulders and the grimaces on their thick, blocky faces. Brothers, maybe.

"Last chance, boys. Leave now and you won't get hurt."

The one in the middle stood watching. "You ain't gonna shoot us or you'd-a done it already. I bet there ain't any bullets in that gun."

So much for the easy way. Colt unslung the rifle and brought it into position. "There's plenty in this one." He flicked the safety to single rounds and aimed. "Now get out of here."

The two on his flanks hesitated and turned to the boy in the middle. He could have been the oldest or the de facto leader or just the biggest bully. Colt didn't care. If he gave in, the others would too.

Come on, leave.

Out of the punk's waistband came a tiny revolver. A .22 or a snub nose .38. A piece with accuracy for shit and a kick a kid couldn't control.

"I'll drop you before you even take a shot."

"Come on Sammy, it ain't worth it."

The kid brought the gun up with one hand, holding it sideways like idiots did on TV.

"He's right. You don't have to do this. Just walk away."

Sammy's thick brow shielded his eyes as he struggled with the decision. Colt kept the rifle aimed at his chest. At this range, the bullet would sail through the kid's chest like a rock through water, but a hit to the heart would still kill.

His finger rested light and easy on the trigger.

The kid stepped back.

Colt exhaled. Maybe this would end well after all. As the kid retreated another step, a metallic clink and slide echoed behind Colt. The restaurant's rear door was opening. *Shit.*

"Hey, Colt. You out here? It's my turn to stand watch."

The kid with the gun panicked, backpedalling into the dark as he took aim on the rear of the building.

"Get back inside!" Colt shouted, but he knew it was all over.

He aimed at the kid's chest and fired, but it was too late. The revolver discharged. The booming echo of the shot bounced off of the metal dumpster and carried into the night.

The kid on the left screamed. The kid on the right turned and ran. Sammy still stood, head bent to inspect the hole in his chest. "You shot me. You bastard." He brought the gun back up, but Colt fired before he had a chance. This time he ended it with a shot to the head.

Sammy crumpled to the ground. The one still standing rushed up, falling to his knees at the sight. "No! Sammy, no!" He reached for the body, hands diving into the thickening blood. He turned to look at Colt. "You didn't have to shoot him."

"Yes, I did."

"He's my brother. You shot my brother."

"Your brother tried to kill me."

Even in the moonlight Colt could see the snot and tears streaming down the boy's face. "He was backing up. He was gonna leave."

"I gave him plenty of chances."

The door to the restaurant banged open again. "What's going on? Doug, are you…? Oh, no." Melody rushed up, but Doug grabbed her by the waist and held her back. "We have to help him."

"It's too late. He's dead." Colt never took his eyes off Sammy's brother. The kid was still a threat and the gun his brother used was a foot away.

"Get the gun, will you, Doug?"

Doug let his sister go and took a step forward, but the kid lunged for it. Colt didn't hesitate. He put two quick rounds in the space between his eyes. He died before he hit the ground.

This time Melody didn't scream. She fainted instead.

DAY THIRTY-TWO

CHAPTER THIRTEEN

MELODY

Chili's
  Springfield, Oregon
  6:00 a.m.

The cup of coffee in her hand did nothing to stop the shaking. Flashbacks of her fight with Captain Ferguson flashed before her eyes. His hands on her body. The menacing look in his eyes. What he intended to do.

She remembered the way his body jerked with each bullet. How he fell to the ground with life still in his eyes. She'd stood up and hobbled away from the first and only man she'd killed and carried on.

The horror of that moment would always stay with her, but it was nothing compared to this. She glanced up at Colt, sacked out on a makeshift bed across the room. The man shot a pair of kids in cold blood and he slept like he'd just had a boring day at the office.

It turned her stomach.

Her brother eased into the chair beside her. "How are you?"

She cut him a glance.

"Ouch. That good, huh?" He sighed and scooted his chair a bit closer. "Don't be so hard on Colt. He did what he had to do."

"No, he didn't. Shooting that kid wasn't necessary. He could have taken the gun from him and let him go."

"You weren't there, Melody. Not at first."

"And you were?" She eyed her brother. He looked like he'd been on a three-day bender. Black circles clung beneath his eyes and his skin took on a sallow tone. "You didn't see the whole thing."

He rubbed his eyes as if to rid himself of the memory. "You need to lay off Colt."

"Why?"

Doug waited until she met his eyes. "Because it was my fault. I'm the reason those two kids are dead."

"What?" Melody couldn't keep her voice low. "I didn't see you with a gun in your hand. You're not the one who shot first."

His jaw ticked as he forced out the words. "I came outside like an idiot, banging the door open and calling out to Colt." Doug swallowed hard. "I spooked the kid with the gun. He fired into the dark. The bullet hit a foot from my head and blasted concrete dust all over me. Colt was protecting me."

Melody glanced back at Colt. Her voice must have carried because he wasn't sleeping anymore. He sat on the edge of the bed, watching her.

She turned back to her brother. "I don't believe you."

"It's true. If he hadn't shot the first kid, then who knows what would have happened. I could be dead. So could Colt. He did the right thing."

Melody pursed her lips. "What about the second one? I was there for it. You could have disarmed him."

"Not if he got to the gun first." Doug reached out and took Melody by the arms. His fingers dug in but didn't hurt. "The world is different now, Mel. You should understand that."

She shook him off. "*I do.*"

"Not well enough."

Melody snorted and turned away. On some level her brother had a point, but she couldn't shake the feeling that Colt had a choice and he opted for the wrong one. Taking a person's life should be the absolute last resort. It wasn't like choosing which socks to put on or whether to bike or drive to work.

She glanced up at Colt. He still sat in the same spot, his expression stoic and unreadable. Was this the way the world worked now? Take someone's life before they take yours? Shoot first and don't bother to ask questions?

If they had never taken Colt and Dani in, she would still be in Eugene, in her own house, sleeping in her own bed. Not dirty and tired and living like a criminal. A yip sounded from a booth a few tables away and Melody turned. Will and Lottie were playing tug with a dishtowel.

Lottie.

Even if she'd stayed in Eugene, she wouldn't have been safe. At some point a militia member would have found Lottie. And then what would have happened to her? Lottie would be dead. Melody would have been rounded up.

If the bedroom they threw her into was anything to go by, she'd have been forced into unspeakable things sooner or later anyway. Melody rubbed at her face. It was all so unreal.

Maybe Doug was right. Maybe she had to accept that killing was a fact of life now, like peeing behind a bush or in a pit dug in the ground, or using gray water to rinse the grime from her hair.

She wanted to believe otherwise, but the more she thought about it, the more unsure she became of everything. The fate of Oregon, the Pacific Northwest, all of America. Was this same scene playing out all across the country? Were other ordinary people struggling with who to let live and who to kill? How to eat and sleep and not die?

Melody stood up and headed over to Colt. She stopped a few feet away and eased into a chair. He regarded her with calm interest.

She tugged at the corner of her shirt. "I'm sorry I gave you a hard time earlier. I know you were protecting us."

He nodded but didn't speak.

"You have so much more experience with taking another person's life. I guess I'm just having a hard time coming to terms with it."

"It never gets any easier."

"It doesn't?"

Colt ran a hand over his head and pinched the back of his neck. "The day ending another person's life becomes easy is the day I put a bullet in my own skull. It doesn't matter if I've been trained to pull the trigger, Melody. I'm still human. I still feel it." He put his fist over his heart. "Right here."

"Then why do it?"

"Because I want to keep living. It's as simple as that." Colt stood up with a grimace and headed toward the kitchen.

Melody watched him walk away.

"That man has put his life on the line for you more times than I can count. I'm not sure questioning his humanity is the right way to say thank you." Larkin stopped beside her chair and offered his hand.

She took it with a frown and stood up. "That's not what I was doing."

"When you ask a former SEAL why he kills people, that's exactly what you're doing."

Melody bristled. "I wasn't questioning his military service."

"He killed those young men last night for the same reason he killed insurgents on active duty. To protect the freedom everyone in this country takes for granted. Just now it's on a more localized scale."

"That doesn't mean I have to like it."

"I sure as hell hope not."

Melody stared up at Larkin. He'd always been so quick to lighten the mood or change the subject before.

But he was all grim stares and hard lips now. She didn't want to fight with him or Colt.

After a moment, she tried to smile, but her lips wouldn't cooperate. "Is it too much to ask for an uneventful day?"

Larkin relaxed and his whole face changed. The hard angles were gone. "You can always ask. Whether it'll happen… that's above my pay grade." He gave her shoulder a squeeze as he walked away.

Melody exhaled and the weight of the night before settled on her shoulders. She didn't know if she would ever get used to this new way of living or if she would struggle with every heartbreaking decision and terrible choice. She stood alone in the little corner of the restaurant, thinking about the future and her place in it until Will called out.

"Melody! Come quick! You'll never believe what they're doing with the Humvee!"

She smiled at his enthusiasm and followed his bounding form toward the rear of the restaurant and the scene of last night's horrible nightmare. Part of her wished she could be as innocent and naive as Will. But she wondered, how long would she survive before reality snuffed her out?

CHAPTER FOURTEEN

DANI

CHILI'S
Springfield, Oregon
7:00 a.m.

"THAT THING WILL REALLY RUN ON NASTY OIL?"

Colt shrugged as the used fryer oil slugged into the gas tank of the Humvee. "Not forever. It'll get us a couple hundred miles, though, before the filters clog. We might make it all the way to Tahoe."

"Why not keep searching for diesel?"

"We've canvassed at least a mile in every direction. We're in the middle of a residential area. There aren't any trucks to siphon."

Larkin set down the empty jug and picked up the next one while Colt held the funnel ready. "If we find some diesel on the road, we can mix it. That'll buy us more time before everything gums up and quits."

"I thought you could run a diesel on vegetable oil no problem." Doug walked out of the restaurant carrying an armful of water bottles. "One of the firefighters I used to work with was always talking about how he wanted to drive around smelling like a French fry."

Colt answered without turning around. "The engine can handle it, but the intake valves and the filters can't. To run unfiltered oil like this, the Humvee needs an adaptor kit we don't have. Like I said, it'll run, just not forever."

Dani watched Colt and Larkin pour the rest of the used oil into the tank in silence. They couldn't leave without another vehicle. Not if they wanted to take the food from the restaurant, the water, and the empty containers for fuel.

She glanced behind her at the street in the early morning light. After Colt's run-in the night before, the sooner they hit the road, the better. She pulled the rifle off her shoulder and walked up to Colt. "I'm gonna scout for a car."

He stood up and wiped his hands on a rag. "Are you sure? Larkin and I can handle it."

"I'm going crazy standing around. Let me do it."

After a moment, Colt nodded. "All right. But as soon as you see something promising, come back and let us know."

She nodded and headed toward the road without another word. Melody and Will stood off to the side, watching Colt and Larkin finish up. Black circles cast deep shadows under Melody's eyes, and Dani wondered if she'd come to terms with what happened in the parking lot. Dani didn't doubt the necessity of Colt's actions. If he believed those kids were a threat, then he should have shot them.

Their world wasn't an insulated, comfortable bubble anymore. It was rough and dirty and meaner than all get out. She used to wish her life was like Melody's. A nice house, plenty of food in the fridge, a little dog to keep her company. But now she was almost thankful for her mother.

If she hadn't grown up part scavenger, part orphan, she would never be able to make the hard choices now. She would be too much like Melody. When confronted with her own safety, Melody could make the tough choices. But when someone else held the power, she couldn't accept the same outcome. Dani hoped the woman would come around.

She left the restaurant on the corner behind and darted across the road. The house across the street appeared vacant, with foot-tall weeds in the front yard and a broken front step. Dani skirted the house, hugging the siding as she tucked in between a bush and the exterior wall. The street turned residential fast, with nothing but houses as far as she could see.

One of them would have a car.

Taking off for the next house, she paused at the edge of the driveway. A single-car detached garage lurked in the back corner of the lot. Dani hustled toward it, ever mindful of her exposed position. She took cover behind the edge of the structure and searched for a window. *Nothing*.

If she wanted inside, she would have to open the

door. She glanced up. The house appeared dark and quiet, but not obviously empty. No trash strewn about. No broken window or porch swing. To open the garage door, she would have her back to the windows.

Too risky. She pushed on, passing four or five more houses without success. At the next block, another garage caught her eye. The house it accompanied suffered more than the rest. Peeling paint. Cracked concrete, a basketball hoop without a net.

Dani eased around the rear of the building, skirting a knocked-over trash can and pile of decomposing garbage. The air hung thick around her like a wet wool blanket, and she covered her nose against the stench. At least the rain held off.

She ducked low, head barely clearing a row of bushes, and ran for the garage. The door was shut and Dani groaned in frustration. What were the chances a car still sat on a driveway in this neighborhood? From the looks of it, slim to none.

The thugs who took on Colt the night before didn't seem the type to discriminate between houses and restaurants. If something of value remained on this street after the power went out, it was long gone now. She sucked in a breath.

I'll have to risk it.

Dani crouched low against the side of the garage and assessed the danger. Three windows on the back of the house, all dark and apparently empty. Line of sight from the garage door to the street and the house opposite. The wood fence running along the driveway obscured her approach from the house next door, but that didn't bring her much comfort.

I'll be a sitting duck.

With a deep breath, she pushed the rifle on her back and went for it. Darting to the door, she grabbed the black-painted metal handle and pulled. Paint flecked off in her hand, but the door only creaked in protest. She crouched low and tried again, putting her legs and back into the effort. The ancient wood groaned and shook and rose about a half an inch before Dani lost her grip.

She staggered back and gripped her jeans above the knees. Air sawed in and out of her lungs.

One more try. That's all she would allow herself. Dani sucked in a breath, clenched her abs, and heaved. The door wobbled, rose an inch or two, and threatened to fall. But Dani refused to let go. Yanking with all her strength, she shoved the door up high enough to grab the bottom before it fell. With her shoulders and back joining the effort, the lumbering beast finally lifted.

As it rocked back into place above her head, Dani sagged to her knees. Her lungs burned, her legs ached, but her eyes widened with hope. The grill of a rusty old pickup sat a foot from her face. She lurched upright and stumbled forward, gripping the dusty front fender for support as she eased around the vehicle.

It hadn't been driven in weeks, maybe months. A thin layer of dust and grime covered every inch. Dani wiped the crud off the dashboard with her sleeve. All dials, no computers. Had to be way older than her. Maybe older than Colt. She slid over and poked around the driver's seat. No seatbelt.

No keys.

It didn't matter. Lack of keys wasn't much of an obstacle. She had to get the thing started. No way was she leaving it here for someone else to find while she ran back to get Colt or Larkin. She clambered out and glanced around the garage. *Please be here, please.*

All she needed was a tool chest. Dodging cardboard boxes and piles of frayed towels, she found a cabinet in the back and tugged it open.

She dug through the tools inside, shoving aside pliers and hammers until she found what she needed: a flat-head screwdriver. Dani almost whooped, but managed to keep quiet. She rushed back to the truck and climbed into the driver's seat.

With a good dose of brute force, Dani shoved the edge of the screwdriver under the plastic housing around the ignition and worked it back and forth. The housing popped off, exposing the inner gears. She jabbed the screwdriver into the hole in the center and twisted with all her might.

Come on, come on. The truck turned over but wouldn't start. She pumped the gas and tried again. *Yes!* It coughed and sputtered as it rumbled to life. Dani put the truck in drive and eased out of the garage.

Screw waiting for Colt and Larkin. She could get them a car all on her own. With a grin on her face, Dani pulled out onto the road. She wasn't the most talented driver, but she'd been behind the wheel more times than she could count thanks to her mom's benders. The car theft came courtesy of one boy who thought they could bond over a life of crime.

Never had she thought it would come in handy until now. Dani hit the gas and the truck rumbled down the block, across the street, and into the parking lot at Chili's.

Meandering over the speed bumps, she pulled the truck in at an angle next to the Humvee and killed the engine. Colt lowered his rifle as she opened the driver's-side door.

Dani's smile faltered as she hopped out. "What's wrong?"

"I almost shot you."

"I found us a vehicle."

Colt's frown deepened. "You aren't old enough to drive."

"*Pfft.* Says who? I've been driving since I was thirteen."

"Parking skills need some work." Larkin walked around the truck from the other side. "But good job, kid. Where'd you find it?"

"In a garage a few blocks from here. It was the only vehicle around."

Colt brushed past her and climbed halfway inside. "Where are the keys?"

Dani shrugged. "I don't know. I just popped the ignition. Works in beaters like this all the time."

Larkin raised an eyebrow but said nothing.

Colt poked around the seats before climbing back down. "You should have stuck to the plan and waited for us."

"I didn't want to take the time. Besides, I never would have gotten the garage door back down. Someone else could have stolen it. It was the right call." Dani didn't know why Colt was acting like this. She thought he'd be happy. Proud, even.

At last, he exhaled. "All right. Let's pack up. We need to hit the road."

CHAPTER FIFTEEN

DANI

Highway 58
   Northwest California
   4:00 p.m.

At fifteen years old, Dani had finally left the state of Oregon. So far, California looked a heck of a lot like her home state. Tons of trees, mountains that swooped and swelled, curvy two-lane roads. It wasn't the glamorous escape she saw on TV.

It wouldn't ever be that again. According to Larkin, the cities were in chaos. Sacramento had been barricaded and left to burn, San Francisco was worse. There would be nothing left of Hollywood.

She leaned forward in the Humvee and squinted. Colt drove the pickup in front, with Harvey, Gloria, and Will crammed in the bench seat beside him. Dani sat in the front of the Humvee with Larkin behind the wheel and Melody, Doug, and Lottie crammed in the back along with a couple jerry cans for fuel and all the weapons.

Thanks to the pickup bed, they were able to bring the salvageable restaurant food and water along with a ton of other useful items. Everything from dish towels to silverware.

The only problem was the Humvee's filters. Thanks to the vegetable oil, the vehicle clunked and sputtered and the gap between them and Colt widened throughout the afternoon. Now Colt cruised about a half a mile ahead. They caught glimpses of him now and then, but the gap made Dani uneasy. Larkin didn't seem to mind.

She stared at the trees ahead. "How far are we from Tahoe?"

"About a hundred and fifty miles. We should be coming up on Lake Almanor soon."

Dani glanced at Larkin. "Will we make it?"

He sat up in his seat and examined the dashboard. "Maybe."

"Should we stop and let the Humvee cool down?"

"No. I'm afraid if we kill the engine it won't start up again. We'll have to drive until it gives out."

Great. Dani turned back to the window. Were road trips always like this? Miles and miles of never-ending forest with nothing to do but stare out the window? She propped her chin in her hand and her gaze wandered.

She blinked. The first time she only caught a glimpse and figured she must be imagining things. The second time, she bolted upright and squinted into the trees. "There's another road! Just through the trees!"

Larkin shrugged. "Probably a logging road."

"I don't think so. There's a car on it. It's keeping up with us."

"You're seeing things. Probably just a reflection off the mirror."

Dani shook her head. "I know what I saw. There's a car over there. Silver or gray. It's tailing us, Larkin."

He glanced over, but didn't take his eyes off the road long enough to confirm her suspicions. "Keep watching. Tell me what type of car and what they're doing."

She spun on him. "I can't see anything but a blur. We need to warn Colt."

Larkin's lips thinned into a line. "If someone's tailing us, then it's too late. Anything I do will put whoever's over there on notice."

"So?"

"Right now they're just watching. If they know we're onto them, it could escalate fast."

Dani slumped back in the seat. "So you're going to do nothing? Colt's in a beat-up old truck. At least we're protected."

Larkin snorted. "No we're not. This isn't an up-armored Humvee, Dani. It's regular issue."

"What do you mean?"

"It's a metal can on wheels. We have no protection."

Dani swallowed. All this time she thought they were basically driving a tank that could go through anything. Bullets. Fire. A throng of angry people. Turned out she was wrong.

Melody scooted forward and popped her head between the front seats. "Why does the army drive this thing if it isn't protected?"

Larkin puffed out his cheeks as he exhaled. "A million reasons. Budget, mostly. But time to produce, weight to transport, ease of use, too. Long story short, we're no better off than Colt and Harvey up there. Maybe a fair bit worse."

Melody retreated into the back and Dani turned her attention to the tree line. The false sense of security she'd held onto for the entire drive disappeared. Unease and fear took its place. She squinted, hoping to catch a glimpse of the foreign car.

Nothing.

Settling into a scrunched-up ball with her knees on the seat, she kept her face an inch from the window. After another thirty miles of nothing, she gave up. "Whoever I saw is gone. Either the road curved away from the highway or they left."

"Good. Because I've got to take a leak." Larkin hit the horn three times and slowed the Humvee. He pulled it over into the grassy shoulder and put it in park. "Keep it running, will you?"

Dani nodded as Larkin hopped out.

"I've got to stretch my legs." Doug clambered out onto the edge of road.

"Lottie needs to go, too." Melody thrust the little dog out the open door and Doug took her before helping his sister.

Dani stayed inside. She focused on the road up

ahead. Colt should be turning around. He had to hear the horn. He wouldn't leave them behind.

"Come on, Lottie. I know you need to go." Melody's voice carried through the open doors, but Dani tuned her out.

Where is Colt? She stood up and leaned across the driver's seat. "Can any of you see the pickup?"

Larkin traipsed out of the tree line and batted at the overgrown weeds. He stopped on the edge of the road. "Not yet. But I hear it, don't you?"

Dani couldn't hear anything over the rumbling, choking engine of the Humvee. "Is he coming?" Something about the entire situation put Dani on edge. She needed to see Colt, alive and well, driving the pickup truck right back their way. "Anything?"

Larkin stepped closer to the road. "Not yet." He motioned to the others. "Get back in. We need to hurry in case he didn't hear us."

As Melody hoisted herself up into the back, the first glint of sunshine on paint caught Dani's eye. The pickup truck bounced into sight, four heads illuminated by the afternoon sun. She exhaled in relief. They were okay. They were coming back.

Larkin waved once to let them know they were safe and heading out. Colt slowed the pickup. He waved in response and swung in a wide arc, turning the truck around.

As Doug eased into the back, Larkin swung the driver's-side door shut. He fell inside with a smile. "Let's see if we can keep up this time, shall we?"

He punched the gas pedal and the Humvee lurched

forward. They trailed Colt's pickup by about a hundred yards. As the truck rounded the corner in front of them, it disappeared behind the trees. Larkin cranked the wheel, following Colt as best he could.

Dani eased forward in the seat, the momentary reprieve of seeing Colt now gone. The Humvee grumbled around the corner and the trees thinned. Two hundred yards ahead, another road crossed the highway. Colt barreled along toward it, the pickup chugging along despite the four passengers and gear in the back.

Larkin cursed under his breath and pumped the gas pedal. They slipped further behind. "Can't you make it go any faster?"

"Nope. This is it and we're getting slower."

He focused on the dash as Dani turned back to the road just as the sun hit chrome. "Larkin!" She jabbed a finger toward the trees. "The other car. It's back!"

"Where?"

"The cross street and coming fast."

Larkin hit the horn. *Beep. Beep, beep, bbbbbeeeeeeeppppppp.* Colt's brake lights lit up.

Dani shook her head. "He can't stop in the intersection! He's got to stop now!"

Larkin pressed down on the horn again, holding it on as he pushed the Humvee to catch up. It wasn't enough.

The silver car that had tailed them for miles burst into the clearing. Everything slowed. The breeze. The tires chewing up asphalt. The sleek silver muscle car as it headed straight for the pickup.

Colt cranked the wheel. The muscle car screeched.

Too little, too late.

The car entered the intersection from the right while Colt banked hard to the left. The front fender of the car hit the truck smack in the middle. Metal crumpled. Backpacks and water bottles flew into the air. The truck's tires came off the ground, but the car didn't stop.

It drove on like a battering ram, upending the pickup and sending it rolling and flipping over the ground again and again. Every time the wheels hit, the truck bounced, up and over, flip after flip.

Dani stared in horror.

Crumpled hunks of metal and food flew off in every direction. A jug of water. A can of apples. The tailgate.

The trees finally stopped the truck's relentless roll. It slammed into a stand of evergreens with a sickening crunch and dropped to the ground.

Dust plumed around it.

The car sat in the middle of the intersection, hood crumpled, but otherwise intact. Dani couldn't breathe. Could anyone survive a crash like that?

Larkin threw the Humvee in park and jumped out, rifle in his hands. "Check the truck. I'm searching the road."

Dani ran after him, her heart hammering like a death toll in her head.

CHAPTER SIXTEEN

COLT

Highway 58
Northwest California
5:00 p.m.

"How much longer?" Will leaned over his grandfather's lap to look out the window. "We've been driving in trees for hours."

Harvey smiled. "We're in California, so probably another three or four."

Gloria twisted around in the seat next to Colt. "Will the Humvee make it? They keep falling behind."

Colt glanced up in the rearview mirror. "I hope so." The last time Larkin pulled over, Colt almost hadn't heard the horn. If they drifted too far apart, he might not know when the Humvee stalled. He eased his foot off the gas and let Larkin catch up.

"There's got to be a place near here for gas. We're coming up on some towns, aren't we?"

Harvey nodded. "Should be soon. We're on the downward slope toward Lake Almanor now. There's a small town there. Tourist-type place."

"We haven't been there in twenty years. Who knows what it's like now."

Colt glanced at Gloria. If that was true, they might as well be heading into the area blind. Twenty years was a long time in Northern California. Whole towns could transform from sleepy little hideouts to destination spots. Colt had lived in Sacramento long enough to see it happen to nearby places like Solvang and Auburn. There was no telling what Lake Almanor and the towns around it were like now.

They needed to be cautious. He glanced at the fuel gauge. It had been stuck on a quarter tank for way too long. Pretty soon it wouldn't matter what kind of town they came across. He would need to siphon some gas.

Colt puffed up his chest and stretched. Riding four across a bench seat didn't give much room for comfort. Gloria almost sat in his lap and poor Will perched on the front of the seat like a bird on a wire. It didn't even have seatbelts.

"As soon as we see some signs of life, we'll need to keep an eye out for gas. Think abandoned cars, farm equipment, motorcycles. Anything with a gas tank that we can siphon."

"What about the Humvee?"

"If it's still running, then diesel or vegetable oil." Colt rubbed at his face and fought off the exhaustion.

After his run-in with the punks the night before, he'd barely slept.

"If you need me to drive, I can take a shift."

Colt turned to thank Harvey when the horn from the Humvee made him pause. The horn sounded again and a burst of chrome and speed flew from the tree line like a silver bullet. *Shit!* Colt cranked the wheel as he slammed on the brakes and Will slid off the seat. The kid's shoulder slammed into the dash as the truck fishtailed.

"Everyone hold on!" Colt screamed and braced for impact. Gloria scrambled for Will. Harvey tried to shield them both.

The pickup didn't stand a chance.

Four thousand pounds slammed into the side of the truck. The bed crushed and crunched and a roll of linens and water jugs flew over the windshield.

The car didn't stop. It kept coming like a beast dredged up from the depths of hell, chewing up asphalt and truck parts as it forced the pickup off the side of the road. The tires hit the dirt, the rubber dug into the weeds, and the world turned on its ear.

Colt fell against the driver's-side door and Gloria landed on top of him. Glass shattered and flew in all directions. Metal buckled all around them but the truck didn't slow down.

It flipped again and Colt slammed into the roof. Pain lanced his shoulder. Glass pelted his face and arms. As the truck rolled down the slope of weeds and dirt, it picked up speed, tossing them about like balls in a bingo machine. Someone's hand smacked him in the face. A foot kicked him in the groin.

They wouldn't survive the crash.

He was going to die right there on some no-name road in the woods of California. Not because someone put a bullet in his head or he'd fought to the end and lost. *No.* A damn car accident. He survived the apocalypse only to be taken out like it was any other day of the week.

As the truck rolled, it caught air, sailing up off the ground. Colt hit what used to be the windshield and kept going. He was free. Flying or falling he couldn't tell which. Air hit him in the face with an accusatory slap. Trees and sky and the promise of the future blurred past him, saying goodbye.

This was the end. He knew it.

Gravity wrenched his body back to earth and he hit the ground so hard, he bounced. When he slammed into the dirt a second time, the world snapped to black.

CHAPTER SEVENTEEN

DANI

Highway 58
    Northwest California
    5:15 p.m.

The truck came to rest on one side in a thicket of young saplings no more than five feet tall. Tree branches stuck through the gaping holes in the frame and the windshield. Smoke billowed from the engine.

Broken bottles and sacks of smashed food littered the scene. Hunks of metal and scraps of plastic dotted the ground. A wet stain coated a shopping bag. *Is that blood?*

Dani scrabbled down the embankment, slipping and sliding on loose rocks and shale as she rushed to the truck. *Be alive. Please, be alive.* She stumbled to a stop a foot from what remained of the truck bed. The tires were shredded. The tailgate had been sheered clean off. A dribble of gasoline leaked from the punctured tank.

She swallowed and stepped closer.

"Let me go first, Dani. It looks like the truck might catch fire." Doug's voice stopped Dani still. In her rush to reach the accident, she'd forgotten he dealt with scenes like this every day.

"What happens if a fire starts?"

Doug glanced up as he picked his way through the wreckage. "Without a fireman's jacket or any gear? We hope to hell we can get everyone out and we run." He disappeared around the front of the truck and Dani held her breath.

A muffled curse carried on the wind.

"Doug?" Melody called out from the road. "Are they alive? Can I help?" She picked her way around the wreckage and stopped within view of her brother before stumbling back. She landed on her butt on the asphalt as the color drained from her face.

Oh, no. Dani couldn't believe it. They weren't all dead. They couldn't be. She rushed forward, heedless of the debris or the risk or Doug's harsh reproach.

"Is Colt—" The sight of a bloody arm, severed at the elbow joint and lying a few feet from the cab, choked off her words. Dani covered her mouth. She recognized Gloria's wedding ring.

From her vantage point, all she could see inside the truck's cab was blood. It splattered against the tan roof and dashboard and dripped over the branches tangled in the windshield. So much freakin' blood. Was Colt in there somewhere? Was his life mixing with that of the Wilkinses as it congealed in the cracked vinyl?

She swallowed down a wave of nausea and regret. What would she do without Colt?

Melody picked her way down the slope and pushed past Dani. "We can't leave them in there. Doug, you have to get them out. You have to try to save…Oh my God."

Doug reached out and grabbed his sister as she sagged to the ground. That afternoon's lunch of oranges and canned beans tumbled from Melody's lips as she heaved into the weeds.

She wiped her mouth with the back of her hand. "Have you checked for a pulse?"

He shook his head. "There's no point, Mel. They're gone."

"Please, Doug. Just do it." Melody gripped her thighs as she heaved again and Doug let her go.

He eased around the side of the truck, bending the stunted trees to make a path. The truck groaned as he climbed aboard the mangled front fender and balanced on one leg as he straddled a hunk of hood. Smoke wafted around him from the engine area, but Doug pressed on, scaling the wreckage until he could grab ahold of the roof.

With one hand gripping where the windshield used to be and one holding fast to a bent side mirror, Doug slipped down into the cab.

Dani waited, holding her breath while Doug maneuvered in the tight space. In the time between watching the crash and now, hope dwindled. The odds of anyone surviving were slim. Nonexistent, maybe. There was nothing left of the truck bed. The cab had been crushed on all sides. The four of them would have to find a way to carry on. They would have to for—

"I've got a pulse!" Doug's shout carried from inside the cab. "Harvey's alive!"

Dani rushed up to the truck and found a foothold on the exposed underside. She hoisted herself up until her fingers found purchase on the door frame. She cleared the side as Doug's head came into view. "What can I do?"

He glanced up in surprise. "We have to get him out, but I don't have any gear. He could have a broken back or neck."

"If we leave him he could bleed out."

Doug frowned. "Even if we get him free of the truck, we can't carry him all the way back to the Humvee."

"We can use the hood of the Camaro." Larkin's voice made Dani jump and she almost lost her footing.

He traipsed out of the trees and stopped on the other side of the truck. "It flew off in the crash and is mostly one piece on the road."

Doug nodded. "That might work. Dani, can you and Melody get it?"

She nodded and climbed down from her perch before grabbing Melody and heading for the road. Dani spotted the silver metal a hundred feet down the pavement. She jogged to it with Melody on her heels. If Harvey was still alive, maybe Colt was, too.

Together the two women dragged the hood down

the embankment. It slipped and skidded and almost cut
Dani's finger off, but they managed. As Doug and
Larkin pulled an unconscious Harvey from the cab,
Melody held the makeshift litter steady.

Blood coated the side of Harvey's head, but he
didn't appear to have any other injuries. The second
Doug set Harvey down, she asked the question burning
a hole in her heart. "Is Colt dead?"

Doug shook his head. "I don't know. He's not in
the truck."

Her eyes widened. "Are you sure?"

Larkin stood up and wiped his bloody hands on his
pants. "He's not on the road. He must have been thrown
from the truck when it flipped. Driver's dead in the car
or about to be."

Dani didn't wait another second. She climbed back
up the embankment and began a search, scanning this
way and that every step, searching for any sign of Colt.
If he was out there, she would find him.

Bits of metal and shards of glass glinted in the
afternoon sun and Dani sidestepped the biggest pieces.
Debris covered the asphalt, but nothing showed signs of
life. Every step brought her closer to the muscle car. It
sat upright, crumpled in on itself, but not destroyed.

Dani approached with caution. Could Colt have
been thrown back toward it? She didn't understand
force or velocity or any of those physics terms she
glossed over in class. As far as she knew, he could be
anywhere, bleeding out while she searched in the wrong
places.

She eased up to the car. Broken valves and tubes

hissed as the car cooled. The driver's-side door hung open forty-five degrees. A boot was perched on the road.

Dani froze. Was the driver still alive? She eased the rifle off her shoulder and checked the safety. They were running so low on ammo. A bullet was now worth more than food or water. *Only fire if desperate.*

Stepping slowly enough not to make a sound, Dani cleared the driver's door. A man was slumped in the driver's seat like Larkin said. Blood pooled on the asphalt by the door and dripped off a jagged wound in his arm. *Plop. Plop. Plop.*

A beard coated his jaw and his neck, hiding pale skin and a sagging wattle. Dani stepped closer. She poked his shoulder with the barrel of her rifle.

He groaned.

Crap. All the time she'd stared at his body, she wished for a corpse. From the amount of blood spreading across the ground, she wouldn't have that long to wait. She eased closer. Empty passenger seat. Dani bent to see past the driver.

What is that?

She leaned closer. *Luggage.* Piles of duffels sat in the back seat, one on top of the other. Anything could be inside. Drugs. Money. Guns.

Dani glanced at the driver. After the first groan, he hadn't made a sound. His chest barely moved. She examined the passenger side. That side of the car took the worst beating, crumpling in on itself from the impact with the truck.

She couldn't get in any other way but past the driver.

Stepping back, Dani glanced around. Where was Colt? Melody and Doug and Larkin still worked on Harvey on the side of the road, each one bending over the car's hood as they tried to keep him alive.

She needed to get on with her search, but she couldn't leave this man here. What if he had something they could use? What if he woke up and got away? She turned back to face him. Melody would hate her for the thoughts running circles inside her brain, but she couldn't turn them off.

He killed their friends. Whether it was an accident or intentional, Dani might never know, but the truth remained. Gloria and Will and maybe Colt were dead because of this man. She didn't need to agonize over the decision. Dani brought the rifle up and aimed at the man's head.

No. She wouldn't waste a bullet. She lowered the gun and reached into her pocket for a hunting knife. One of the few things she'd managed to save from Colt's haul at the sporting goods store in Eugene. She'd kept it in her pocket ever since the run-in with Jarvis and Captain Ferguson.

It had always been a weapon of last resort. Now it would be her first choice. Dani flicked out the blade. Four inches long and sharpened to slice through a kill like hot butter. She eased up to the driver. Sucked in a breath.

This is the right call. I'm doing the right thing. She shut down her emotions and her nerves and forced her panic to subside. *I can do this.*

One quick jab and twist and even if the bastard woke up, he'd never make it. Dani exhaled and stepped closer.

"What the hell are you doing? Trying to get yourself killed?"

Dani spun around. Colt stood ten feet behind her, using a tree branch as a crutch.

"You're alive!"

"Seems that way." He winced instead of smiled. "But my knee is jacked up and my brain auditioned for a spot on a roller derby team."

"Did your brain make it?"

He snorted and hobbled toward her. "Is he alive?"

She nodded. "For now."

Colt pulled his Sig Sauer from his holster. "I'd step back."

Dani did as she was told and watched as Colt pulled the trigger. The gunshot echoed down the street and the second he lowered the gun, she rushed him.

Her arms made it three-quarters of the way around his shoulders. "I thought you were dead."

"Me, too." Colt hugged her back with one hand as Larkin stopped beside them.

Dani pulled back and wiped at her face.

"Anything I should know?"

Colt tilted his head. "I'm alive and that guy's dead."

Larkin nodded. "So are Gloria and Will. Harvey's hanging on, but I don't think for that much longer."

Colt sagged. "I saw it too damn late."

Dani spoke up. "Did you see them tailing us?"

"What?"

Dani glanced at Larkin. "I don't know if it was the same car, but I caught a glimpse of one on a frontage road. It stayed with us for a while, then disappeared."

Colt shook his head. "We were too far ahead of you. I didn't see it. Do you think the same one?"

"Maybe."

Larkin clapped Colt on the back. "Either way, there was nothing you could do. It was barreling through the intersection. Had to be going a hundred, maybe more."

Colt nodded. "Still sucks."

"You're damn straight." Larkin stepped up and eased his shoulder under Colt's arm and took the tree branch. "Let's get you checked out. Melody's about done with Harvey."

Dani stood beside the car, hesitating.

"Are you coming?"

She glanced at the dead man. "There's one thing I want to check out."

"Be careful, Dani."

She watched Colt and Larkin shuffle away before turning back to the car. Holding her breath, she crawled over the man who now sported a bullet hole in the center of his forehead. He stank like beer and bodily fluid.

With one hand on the seat, she reached out for the closest duffel. It didn't budge. She would have to crawl all the way into the back. Wedging herself between the dead man's thigh and the passenger seat, she managed to crawl in far enough to reach a zipper.

Dani tugged, hoping for something they could use. The bag fell open and her mouth followed suit.

CHAPTER EIGHTEEN

COLT

Highway 58
Northwest California
7:00 p.m.

EVERYTHING HURT. COLT TILTED HIS HEAD TO THE right and his brain sloshed like unset Jell-O. He waited for the world to stop spinning.

"You're damn lucky to be alive. I scoured the pavement looking for body parts." Larkin plopped down on the asphalt next to Colt. "Didn't expect to find you in one piece."

"I bounced around inside the cab like a pinball until the windshield shattered. One of the rollovers must have thrown me out."

"I'm surprised you're not impaled on a branch or head-first in the middle of a tree trunk."

Colt rubbed at his sore shoulder. "Feels like I did

both, but I came to facedown in a weedy ditch. If it had kept raining, I'd have drowned in the muck."

Larkin held up his hand. "How many fingers?"

Colt squinted. "Too many to count."

"You've got a concussion, that's for sure."

"I've lost more brain cells than Mayweather last season."

Larkin chuckled. "At least your sense of humor's still intact."

Colt grew somber. "I tried to avoid the Camaro. It came on so fast, I couldn't—" He glanced at Melody's hunched-over form behind him, wincing as his back twisted. "I should have seen it."

He thought about Gloria and Will and their last moments on earth. Fear and pain and agony. He didn't wish it on anyone. And now Harvey clung to life. Even if he did survive, once he found out his wife and grandson were dead…

"Stop beating yourself up. We watched the whole thing. It was unavoidable."

"I should have done more."

"Unless one of those bullets you've stopped lately infused you with super powers, you did all you could."

Colt rubbed his eyes. He knew Larkin spoke the truth, but it didn't matter. Gloria and Will would stay with him. After surviving Jarvis and the house fire and an assault on the militia's stronghold, to die in a car crash didn't seem fair. "How's Harvey?"

"Barely breathing." Larkin leaned back on his hands, his face grim. "Even if we had antibiotics and the best medical care—"

"He wouldn't make it."

"Not a chance."

Colt exhaled. "Does Melody know?"

Larkin glanced at the makeshift litter where Harvey still lay unconscious. "If she does, she won't admit it."

"Doug?"

"He knows. He's not an EMT, but he's seen more car accidents than either of us."

"How long?"

"A few days." Larkin scraped a hand down his face. "But Harvey will be in agony. He's got a broken leg, ribs are smashed all to hell, and there's a nasty gash above his eye. Who knows about internal injuries. If he survives the night, the pain will only increase."

Colt nodded. He'd seen his share of injuries in conflicts as a SEAL. The first few days were cruel in their optimism. Hope bloomed in the inexperienced when sailors with catastrophic injuries regained consciousness and seemed to improve.

When infection set in, everything flipped. Weak smiles turned to screams. Optimism turned to horror and pity. Without a hospital, Harvey would suffer right up until the end. "Do we have anything?"

Larkin knew where Colt was going. He'd been in combat as gritty and violent as anything Colt had experienced. "Not even a bottle of whiskey."

"It's not going to be easy."

"Nothing will." Larkin stretched his feet out in front of him and let his shoulders sag. "If you haven't noticed, we lost all the food."

Colt raised his head. He'd been so focused on the

Wilkins family, he'd not stopped to think about the living. "All of it?"

"We packed it all in the pickup. As soon as the Camaro hit it, the garbage bags went flying. Everything canned exploded on contact with the road, the potatoes splattered, the water jugs burst." He shook his head. "We might be able to salvage a handful of oranges, but—"

"They were almost rotten to begin with."

Larkin nodded.

Colt glanced up at the darkening sky. "So we're up shit creek."

"Without a paddle."

No food. No water. A handful of bullets and a man too injured to move. Not a recipe for success. Colt didn't know what to do. Ordinarily he was a take-charge kind of guy. A problem was a challenge to solve, not an insurmountable obstacle. But he'd never been faced with something so grim.

Missions ended. They failed or succeeded and he was either extracted or they'd recover his body. But there was always someone out there, somewhere, who had his back. Not this time. They were on their own.

No stores. No aid. No government to help them. Colt, Larkin, Dani, and the Harpers would live or die on the backs of their wits and strength. Nothing more.

He pushed himself off the ground, wincing with the effort. "How much farther can the Humvee go?"

Larkin stood and focused on the tan beast of a vehicle. "No more than fifty miles, I'd say."

Great. Add no real transportation to their list of bad

news. "Then I guess we're making camp. We can all pile in the Humvee for the night to stay warm. Set out in the morning."

"Harvey won't fit. One of us will have to stay with him and keep watch."

"There isn't any way to get him in there?"

"Moving him is a bad idea. If his back is broken—"

Colt held up a hand. He knew the drill. "Then we need shelter and we need it fast. There are enough trees around here. We can strip some branches and make a lean-to."

Larkin nodded. "I'll ask Doug to help."

As he turned toward the woods, Dani caught his eye. She lurched toward them, half-carrying, half-dragging a duffel bag along behind her. She stopped in front of them both and dumped the bag on the ground.

"What's in the bag?"

She wrapped a hand around her middle as she sucked in a few lungfuls of air. "Open… it."

Larkin crouched and unzipped the bag. "Whoa. You see this, Colt?"

Colt bent to inspect the contents. "There have to be twenty guns in there." He counted a dozen Glocks of various sizes, an armful of rifles beneath them. Even a few defensive shotguns for good measure. He stood up in a rush and the ground wobbled. "Where'd you find these?"

Dani jerked her thumb toward the smashed-up car. "In the backseat of the bastard that hit you. There's four more just like it still in there. A bunch of ammo boxes, too."

Colt met Larkin's heavy stare. They were thinking the same thing. No one transported this much weaponry by themselves. A few dozen guns and hundreds of rounds of ammo? Not a chance. The dead man in the Camaro was now a much bigger problem.

"Get Doug to help you unload the car. Take all the duffels and ammo boxes to the Humvee and load them in the back."

"What are you going to do?"

Colt and Larkin stood up at the same time. "Figure out the best way to get rid of the evidence."

Dani scrunched her eyebrows. "I don't understand."

Larkin filled her in. "Someone right now is wondering where the hell their guns are at. That man wasn't driving an arsenal at a hundred miles an hour because he needed to get some fresh air."

"He was meeting someone."

Colt nodded. "And now he's late."

The implication washed over Dani's face and she paled. "They'll be looking for him."

"Exactly. If we don't hide the car, we'll be sitting ducks."

"We should just pack up and go. We can cram everything in the Humvee and hit the road."

"Harvey can't travel."

Dani's eyes went wide. "We can't stay here! If someone is coming to find this guy, we'll be right in their path."

Colt rubbed the back of his neck. "We've got plenty of defenses, now. We'll be all right."

"You can't be serious."

"About what?" Doug stopped next to Dani. He almost jumped when he spotted the duffel of guns at their feet. "What the hell is that?"

Larkin motioned at the crashed car. "The asshole's payload."

Doug glanced at the Camaro and back at Larkin. "He was a weapons smuggler?"

"Transporter, at least."

Doug's gaze bounced back and forth between the guns and Colt and Larkin. "We need to leave. Whoever wants those weapons will be coming."

"What about Harvey?"

Doug whipped his head toward his sister and Harvey's unconscious form. "If we move him, he'll die."

It was as bad as Colt feared. If they stayed they would be sitting ducks. If they left, they would be condemning Harvey to death. He focused on Doug's face as he asked the only important question. "Does Harvey have any chance of pulling through?"

Doug didn't hesitate. "Yes. He does."

The answer surprised him. If there was a chance… Colt made up his mind. "I'll stay here with Harvey. The rest of you pack up and move out."

"No way." Dani crossed her arms. "I'm staying, too."

Larkin chimed in. "The kid's right. I'm not leaving you here to get yourself killed."

"We can't leave. If whoever wants those guns does show up, you're a sitting duck. Instead of saving Harvey, you'll be killing both of you." Doug's lips thinned. "We all stay until Harvey is safe enough to travel."

Colt exhaled. He didn't like the idea one bit. "We'll need shelter. A lean-to big enough for at least Harvey and one other person. There might be a tarp from the truck or branches we can use."

"We can move the Humvee into the trees. Add some branches to camouflage it."

"What about the car?" Dani chewed on her lip as she waited for Colt's answer. So young, but so capable.

He ran a hand down his face. "Can you unload it?"

She nodded.

"Good. Get everything out and we'll push it down the road. I've got an idea." Colt didn't like staying. It was setting them up for an ambush. He hoped his plan would put whoever came looking off their trail, but he didn't have a lot of faith.

If it didn't work, they'd be forced to run or take a stand.

DAY THIRTY-THREE

CHAPTER NINETEEN

MELODY

Highway 58
Northwest California
2:00 a.m.

Her teeth banged together in a relentless chatter and Melody hugged her sweater tighter against the chill. Harvey hadn't so much as groaned despite the temperature dropping at least twenty degrees in the night. Melody didn't know what to do.

She checked Harvey's pulse every five minutes and confirmed his lungs still filled with air, but that was it. Without any drugs, she couldn't alleviate his discomfort or ward off infection or even reduce the swelling. His right ankle looked like a grapefruit and she couldn't even ice it.

A sob slipped out between her chattering teeth and

Melody shoved her fist against her mouth. *What a naive fool I've been.*

She brushed her fingertips across Harvey's forehead. Still hot. At some point in the night, his body gave in to a fever and now he radiated more heat than an electric blanket. It wasn't enough to keep her warm, but the cold air wasn't hurting him.

Melody wiped at her face. Gloria and Will were dead. Doug and Larkin moved their bodies to a restful spot among the trees, but they weren't buried. Their lifeless forms just lay on the ground, open for birds and squirrels and mice to run all over.

She closed her eyes and the accident replayed in her mind. So fast and deadly. And now they were trapped a hundred feet off the road in a makeshift camp while Harvey struggled to keep breathing.

They would never make it somewhere safe. They would never be comfortable again. Hunger roiled her belly, but Melody shoved it down. She couldn't think about food while Harvey died a slow and agonizing death before her eyes.

The cut tree branches beside her rustled and Lottie rushed in. The little dog jumped into Melody's arms as Larkin eased into the makeshift first aid tent. "Thought you could use some company."

Melody tried to smile. "Thanks."

He held out a cup full of steam. "Pine needle tea. It won't fill you up, but it'll curb your appetite."

She took it with a nod and wrapped her fingers around the mug. "Where'd you find this?"

Larkin shrugged. "I've been scouring the forest for

our gear. One box of dishes wasn't a complete loss. And I found a jug of water still half full. The mud slowed the leak." He squeezed into the space between Melody and the wall. "The potatoes weren't so lucky."

Melody snorted. "You should get some sleep."

"Can't. Colt snores like a beached walrus."

"You're familiar with their sound?"

"Tons of them on the beach when I was stationed in Alaska. Real pains in the ass, too. Always complaining and barking orders." He smiled. "Not that different from the army, now that I think about it."

Melody scowled. "How can you make jokes? Gloria and Will are dead, Harvey's barely hanging on. We've lost all our food, the Humvee is about to give up, and we're lost in the middle of nowhere."

"Don't forget, we're hiding from a bunch of bad guys, too."

Melody punched Larkin in the arm. "I'm serious."

"I am, too. Whoever ordered those guns isn't going to let a missing shipment go. They'll be coming."

Melody forced the question out. "What do we do?"

"As soon as Harvey can move, we leave."

"You mean as soon as he's dead."

Larkin glanced at her, an unreadable expression on his face. "How long does he have?"

"I don't know."

"Then we need to make the most of it." He stretched his legs out in front of him and leaned back against a tree trunk. "Tell me your favorite memory of Harvey and Gloria."

Melody blinked. "Why?"

Larkin reached out and gave her arm a squeeze. "Because Harvey's not dead yet and maybe hearing about his life will help the man find his way home."

Melody glanced at Harvey. The man had been her neighbor for as long as she could remember. But a favorite memory? She thought in silence before it came to her. A small, sad smile tilted the corners of her mouth. "One year when I was a teenager, Harvey asked if we could help him pick out a Christmas tree."

Larkin urged her to continue.

"He had this tradition of traipsing up into the mountains around Eugene and cutting off the top of a Douglas fir." Melody smiled. "He'd shimmy up that tree like a bear after honey. It was scary and funny and completely insane all at the same time."

"Where do you come in?"

"One year Harvey hurt his back. Slipped a disc or something. So he asked Doug to help." She sipped some tea and shook her head. "So there's my city brother, eighteen years old, with a saw and some brand-new boots, traipsing through the December snow."

Larkin grinned. "Doug wasn't much for roughing it back then?"

"Still isn't." She smiled and continued. "Harvey picked some tree that had to be forty feet tall. Doug took one look at it and his eyes went all wide and he turned to me."

"Did you talk him out of it?"

Melody stifled a quiet laugh. "I told him to get on with it. So he climbed the tree with the saw, got all the way up to ten feet from the top and hacked at it until the top came crashing down."

"What's so funny about that?"

"Doug couldn't get down. He was like a treed cat up there, clinging to the trunk and howling. Harvey shook the tree and scared him so bad he shimmied down. Poor Doug pulled pine splinters out of his hands for a week."

By the time she finished the story, tears of laughter leaked from Melody's eyes. She smiled at Harvey's still body where he lay on the hood of the Camaro.

"Did he ever ask Doug to help him again?"

"Not a chance." She reached forward and rested her hand on Harvey's shoulder. After a minute, she found her voice. "Harvey's a good man. He deserves better than this."

Larkin nodded. "None of us expected to be here, Melody. We've done the best we could."

"Have we?" She turned on him, tone more accusatory than she meant. "Is that really true?" She broke eye contact and focused again on Harvey. "When the power first went out, we did nothing. Just sat back and waited for help to arrive like it always did before. Then when Jarvis took over…"

Larkin shifted beside her. "You could have kept your head down, stayed with the militia. Maybe that would have been better."

"And let them round me up to do God knows what down the road?" She shook her head. "The more I think about it, the more I'm convinced we should have left first thing. I've got friends in Washington state. We could have driven up there and hiked into Canada."

"What makes you think it's better there than it is here?"

"The whole world can't be powerless. Someone somewhere has electricity."

"Stop second-guessing yourself. What's done is done. You can't change the past."

Melody drained the rest of the tea. "I can still be bitter about it."

"Or you can think about the future." Larkin took the empty mug and set it by the tree-branch wall. "The world before the power went out is gone. We need to stop hoping for it to come back and start living now. This right here is what we have."

She snorted. "A crappy lean-to, a dying man, and no food?"

He smiled. "I was thinking more a beautiful woman who has more strength and courage than she gives herself credit for."

Melody stilled. Larkin stared at her with an intensity she'd forgotten existed, and Melody wished they were anywhere else. "You think I'm strong?"

He nodded. "And brave. Stop beating yourself up over what might have been and focus on what you can do *now*."

"It's not that easy."

"Yes, it is." Larkin reached out and trailed his fingers over Melody's cheek.

She shuddered. He leaned forward.

Melody's breath caught in her lungs like a bird in a net, wings unfurled, going nowhere. "I don't think—"

"You're right. Don't think at all. Just act." Larkin's lips hovered an inch away and Melody's eyes slid shut.

She waited, frozen in place as he closed the distance between them.

A low, guttural growl broke the spell and Melody jerked back. Lottie sat on her lap, ears pricked toward the road. Melody glanced up at Larkin in alarm.

He held a finger in front of the lips she almost kissed.

Lottie growled again and Larkin rose onto his feet. "Don't move." He checked the safety on the pistol he carried and ducked out from beneath the makeshift shelter.

Melody stared at the empty space he left behind and shivered.

CHAPTER TWENTY

DANI

Highway 58
  Northwest California
  3:00 a.m.

"Dani, wake up!"

"Go away." Dani swatted at the hand shaking her shoulder. It couldn't be morning already. A gust of cold air made her squirm.

"Wake up. We need to move. There's someone coming."

Dani's eyes flew open. Larkin stood beside the open door to the Humvee, letting in cold air and panic. Reality stole her breath. The car crash. Gloria and Will and Harvey. The guns. She smacked her dry lips together. "Where?"

"Same road as the Camaro, opposite direction."

"How far?"

"Minutes." Larkin glanced behind him. "We need better cover."

She sat up in the seat and rubbed the last bit of sleep from her eyes.

Larkin handed her a rifle. "Find a tree and hide behind it." He pointed at the road. "They're coming from the west. If they spot the Camaro, they'll come at us from this direction."

"When do we engage?"

"Not until we've been spotted. If we're lucky, they'll drive right by us."

Dani didn't feel lucky. She clambered out of the Humvee and hit the ground with both feet. "Where's Colt?"

"Scouting. Doug and Melody are pulling Harvey into some brush. I need you as another shooter. Can you handle it?"

The faint hum of a motor pricked her ear. "Yeah."

"Good." Larkin clapped her on the back and set off toward the crossroad.

Dani loped into the trees. The night air clutched at her bare neck and she shivered. Leaves and branches smacked her face and clawed her jeans as she traipsed into a thicket of dense foliage. The forest smelled of damp earth and decaying logs and she fought the urge to sneeze.

With a full canopy of new leaves, the forest blocked most of the moon. Pale shafts of light filtered through the breaks in the forest, but Dani couldn't make out more than a few feet in any direction. She wouldn't be able to shoot anyone until they were almost on top of her.

Not good.

The low rumble of the car engine grew louder and Dani strained to see the road. *There!* A flash of car headlights through the trees. She eased closer, heading in the direction of the lights. They came in and out of focus like a strobe as the car drove down the crossroad.

The lights hugged the road, low and wide. Not a Humvee or even a truck. Maybe it was a friendly, innocent sedan. An unrelated driver, oblivious to the accident and the cache of guns in the Camaro. Maybe it wouldn't even slow down when it reached the state highway.

Dani ducked behind a large tree trunk and waited twenty feet off the side of the crossroad. The glow from the headlights steadily increased. The twin lights bounced and weaved as they approached the intersection. Dani let herself hope.

Keep going. Keep going.

The headlights wavered and slowed.

She cursed beneath her breath. The car stopped, its lights illuminating the intersection and the scene of the accident. Colt and Larkin had pushed the Camaro into the ditch, but they couldn't do anything to cover it up or hide the pickup. Colt had hoped it wouldn't be seen from the road and any driver would cruise on by. Guess he was wrong.

A low, throaty grumble spread through the forest from the car's idling engine as Dani waited.

The driver's door opened with a squeal and slammed a moment later. A silhouette, stocky and solid, parted the beams of light. Dani shifted in her crouch. They could take on one man, even with Harvey injured and the light working against them.

Another door opened. Another figure cut in front of a headlight. Bigger. Wider. Dani swallowed. *It will be okay.*

She raised the rifle to her eye and took in the size and shape of the two men in the lights. Killing them now would be easy. Two shots a piece, and they would fall like leaves to cold asphalt. Her finger eased around the trigger, but she didn't pull.

What if they were innocent? What if they were merely stopping to find a place to relieve themselves or checking the wreck for survivors? What if the two men standing in the light could help them? Food. Water. A place to sleep.

She frowned. Would her first instinct now always be to shoot first and not bother with questions? Was that her life?

Dani thought about her mother and her life before. When her mother was on a tear or a dealer was after her, Dani never stood up for herself. Instead of fighting back and taking charge, she ran and hid like a coward. She didn't have the strength to fight.

Was shooting these men any different? It was still cowardice. Still fear. She eased her finger off the trigger. With Colt and Larkin in the woods, they could survive even if the men on the street were out for vengeance.

As she leaned back in her crouch, the driver stepped

out of the headlights. Dani watched the beams of light until *bam!* They disappeared.

The forest plunged into darkness, inky thick and impossible to navigate. She stared at those stupid headlights for so long that without them, she was blind. Dani cursed herself again. *Stupid girl.* She'd been so consumed with doing the right thing and all the what-ifs, she didn't stop to think about what would happen next.

The night closed in around her, every sound amplified a million times. A cricket in the leaves at her feet. An owl half a mile away. A crunch of a twig way too close to ignore.

Dani froze.

She couldn't run. She couldn't shoot. There was nothing to do but stay still and hope they couldn't see her. They could still be friendly. They could still be good people.

Fear spiked her heart. It pounded loud enough to drown out the cricket and the owl and a million other sounds. But not the crunching leaves. Not the snapping twigs. Someone was out there and headed straight for her.

What if they caught her? She couldn't let that happen. Dani closed her eyes and breathed in the forest. Dank decay, fresh new leaves. Grease and dirt. A person. She opened her eyes and focused on the smell and the sound. She wouldn't let them catch her. She would take them out even if she couldn't see.

Her finger twitched around the trigger as she pulled the butt of the rifle tight against her shoulder. Tree bark scraped her back through her clothes as she pressed herself against it. *I won't die out here. Not now. Not like this.*

CHAPTER TWENTY-ONE

COLT

Highway 58
   Northwest California
   3:00 a.m.

THE FOREST POSED NO OBSTACLE TO COLT IN THE darkness. His feet rolled over the leaves without a sound. His gun-toting arm tucked close and tight to his chest to avoid a surprise attack. The men standing around the Mustang idling on the road would never hear him above the engine noise.

He eased close enough to assess the threat. Two men. One a beefy two hundred-plus pounds, round from beer and inactivity. The other taller and better conditioned.

From the way both men held shotguns draped across their non-shooting arms, they were skilled in firearm use. They stood in the beam of the headlights, staring at the wrecked Camaro. Colt knew if someone came looking, they would find it.

Dragging the driver's body into the brush had been the right call. Without his body, the men standing in the road didn't know if he'd crashed and run off with the guns himself, been kidnapped, or what. There could be a million different scenarios.

They wouldn't know where to go or what to do. If they headed for the Humvee, Colt would take them out. Otherwise, he planned to leave them alone. Men stockpiling weapons could be useful in a lawless America. Colt didn't want to kill them unless he had a damn good reason.

He stood behind a thick pine, waiting and listening. The passenger loped ahead to the wrecked Camaro and disappeared out of the headlight beam. A few minutes later he clawed back out, shaking his head. If he said anything, Colt couldn't hear it.

The driver stalked back to the car and reached inside the open window. The engine faded into silence. Thirty seconds later, the headlights flicked off. Colt couldn't see, but neither could the two men. They were as blind as he was, maybe worse.

Colt squeezed his eyes shut and used the palms of his hands to put pressure on his eyes. After a count to ten, he released his eyes and blinked back the startling white blindness. Not perfect, but the quick trick improved his vision substantially.

The men had moved away from the car. Colt crept closer. Without the steady hum of the engine, he teased their whispers from the darkness.

"You think Butch took off?"

"With all those guns? That boy couldn't carry a sack of potatoes ten feet. How's he gonna lug fifty rifles?"

"Maybe he buried them."

"Where?"

"He could have put them in the bushes. It's darker than the inside of a cow in that damn forest. He could have stashed them under a log or something."

"We should go back and tell Cunningham. Let him decide what to do."

"And get our asses chewed for not searching the area? You wanna do that, go right ahead, but I'm checking it out."

"With what?"

"There's a flashlight in the glove box. We can poke around at least."

Colt frowned. So far the men hadn't come across the smashed-up truck or the Humvee. But if they started traipsing around in the forest, they *would* find it.

A car door opened and the sounds of rummaging filtered back to Colt. He eased deeper into the forest, hoping to still catch the conversation but not be seen. A weak flashlight clicked on.

"Man this thing's a piece of crap. We'll never find anything with it."

"We can't go back until we try. You know Cunningham. The minute he finds out the guns are gone, he'll flip."

"What do we need them for, anyway? Haven't we got enough?"

"He says there's never enough."

Whoever this Cunningham fellow was, Colt agreed with him. Guns, ammo, food, and water. The four things you could never have too much of. As the two men headed back toward the Camaro, Colt kept pace, slinking behind trees and bushes.

The flashlight beam roved over the smashed-up car and the tree line beyond. The taller man broke the silence. "You think Cunningham's right?"

"'Bout what?"

"All that talk about America being over. That this is the new world."

"The whole, 'we're explorers and can conquer any land we see fit?'"

"Yeah. That."

The shorter man shuffled in and out of the light. "I don't know. Seems a bit kooky to me, but he's done all right, ain't he? We've got food and water and so far no one's come to take it."

"But what's he need all these weapons for? It don't make sense."

"Defense. It must be."

"I don't know. Hey…what's that?" The flashlight caught the dirty chrome of the pickup's smashed bumper. Both men readied their weapons and approached. The beam of light dipped into the ditch off the side of the road.

Colt knew it was only a matter of time, now. The odds of getting out of there without being spotted were rapidly deceasing. He could take the two men out, but he didn't want to unless he had no choice. Their conversation sparked more than interest.

They had food and shelter and tons of weapons. This Cunningham fellow had managed to assemble what sounded like a pretty good setup. Joining a place like that could be the best option. Assuming it was taking any more members.

But he couldn't just walk out of the woods and ask. The two men were liable to shoot on sight. No, Colt needed to find out more about Cunningham and where he set up camp before he brought it up to the rest of the group. If this trek out of Eugene taught him anything, it was the need for more supplies, training, and people.

With only five of them functional and Harvey on his last breath, they would never be able to start over with nothing. Even if he didn't stay in whatever makeshift town these men came from, Doug and Melody might be able to start over. They might find a little piece of what they lost.

Colt closed the distance between him and the two men. The flashlight beam bounced around the cab of the truck and Colt picked up their conversation.

"—too much blood. No way somebody survived this."

"Then where are the bodies?"

"Probably with our guns."

"We need to get back and assemble a team to search. We can't do this on our own."

Colt backtracked into the forest. He needed to find Dani and the rest of them and explain what he heard. They could put following the men to a vote.

A blob of light landed three feet from his boot and he froze.

"You hear that?"

"Probably a deer or something."

"Naw, man. It sounded like a person."

The light swooped over his left shoulder and Colt eased to the ground.

"I'm gonna check it out."

The flashlight bobbed and weaved and Colt pressed closer to the damp forest floor. The light swooped over his back. If they spotted him, it was game over. He would have no choice but to engage.

"Hey! I got something!"

Shit. Colt readied himself for a fight, but the flashlight beam arced away from him.

"It's a military truck! I told you someone was out here!"

Oh, no. As the light bounded toward the Humvee, Colt rose up. He turned and made his way toward the area Larkin had set up as a safety zone. They would need to hide until these idiots got sick of searching. A few feet ahead of him a pale shape floated against a tree.

Colt squinted. *Dani?* He eased closer. The teenager clutched a rifle tight to her body, swooping it back and forth. From the way it quivered, he knew she was terrified. And blind.

He whistled a faint high-pitched note. She swiveled toward him. He took another step. The rifle hung in the air, ready to fire.

"Dani!"

The gun jerked.

"Dani, it's Colt."

She lowered the weapon and he stepped close enough for her to see him in the dark.

"I almost shot you."

"I'm glad you didn't." He motioned for her to crouch and he did the same. "The men found the Humvee. We need to distract them and get out of here."

"How?"

The sound of the Mustang revving caught them both off guard and they spun toward the noise. The headlights flared and the car revved before lurching forward. It spun a one eighty as shouts erupted from the tree line.

The two men charged the car as it shot off in the direction they had come. The headlights lit up the night as the car sped away. Colt tugged on Dani's arm. "Let's go."

"Where?"

"To the Humvee. Larkin's given us a chance."

"What about him?"

"Don't worry. He'll find us."

Colt and Dani took off for the vehicle. They made it just as Melody and Doug emerged from the trees, dragging Harvey behind them.

"What's going on?" Doug heaved the Camaro's hood closer to the Humvee as Colt yanked open the back door.

"Larkin's giving us a chance. Everyone in."

"What about Harvey?"

Colt glanced down at the unconscious man. "Get him in the back."

"But if we move him—"

"We don't have a choice."

Dani rushed to the passenger door while Colt clambered up into the driver's seat. He flipped the switch on the dash and waited as Doug and Melody eased Harvey inside and shut the doors. Colt turned on the Humvee.

It sputtered and cranked and for a moment he wondered if it would turn over, but at last, a weak grumble managed to hold. He eased it into the forest, turned on the headlights, and punched the accelerator. They'd be off-roading it from now on.

CHAPTER TWENTY-TWO

MELODY

Northern California Forest
5:00 a.m.

The Humvee spluttered and lurched. Melody fell against the door and Harvey's limp body slid off the divider. His hand flopped into her lap.

She braced herself as the vehicle straddled a ditch. This couldn't get any worse. The engine coughed and the Humvee seized up as it attempted to crest a hump in the forest. The tires slipped.

Colt cursed from the front seat and revved the engine, but instead of moving forward, the Humvee rolled back. It stopped on level ground, engine hissing. He flipped the switch and pumped the gas. Nothing.

Doug eased forward from the back. "Is that it?"

"Afraid so." Colt twisted around. "The engine is fried. Even if it cools, I don't think it will restart."

Melody reached for Harvey. His head had slid off the divider and it lay at an unnatural angle, his eyes wide open and vacant. With two fingers, she searched for a pulse. Again and again she moved her hand around his neck, fear and denial rising in her throat the longer she searched. Her brother's hand wrapped around her own.

"Mel."

She glanced up. Doug's eyes were full of knowledge and caring. "Is he gone?"

"I can't find a pulse. If we start CPR, maybe—"

"It's best to let him go."

She tore her gaze away from Doug and stared down at Harvey. This couldn't be happening. A month ago, they were all just living their lives. Friends and neighbors waving as they passed on the street, sipping coffee on the front porch on a lazy Saturday morning, chatting about the weather.

Now Harvey was another casualty of this war without an enemy. A man who had already sacrificed his home and everything he owned for strangers to whom he didn't owe anything. It didn't seem fair. The Wilkins family was dead. For what?

Tears pricked her eyes and Melody didn't will them back. One tumbled from the middle of her lash line and splashed across Harvey's lifeless cheek. Gloria had been her friend her entire life, from babysitting when she could barely walk to being a shoulder to cry on after her parents died. Now the woman's body was left to rot in the middle of a forest hundreds of miles from home.

Harvey had been a friend to her father and to Doug.

He deserved better than to die in the back of a Humvee bouncing through underbrush and dry creek beds. He should be sitting at the kitchen table right now, drinking coffee and watching the sunrise.

Melody snuffed back a sob. Her brother squeezed her hand, but she shook him off, anger welling up inside her to replace the grief. "What are we doing out here?"

She looked up at Doug. He'd always been so confident before the power loss. Taking charge and protecting her. Now what could he do? Sit there and stare while Colt figured out what to do next?

Lottie yipped from Dani's lap. The poor dog hadn't eaten a decent meal in days and spent the last night with nowhere to sleep except beside a dying man. Melody reached for her and Lottie scrambled into her arms.

If things continued down this path, soon she would be saying goodbye to Lottie, too.

Colt spoke up from the front. "I'm sorry, Melody."

She snorted and wiped at her face. "Are you really?"

"Mel!"

"What?" She snorted at her brother. "It's a legitimate question."

Colt answered. "Of course I am."

Melody swallowed. Rage simmered below the surface of her body, writhing like a serpent kept too long in a cage.

Rage at Colt for forcing their decision to leave Eugene. Rage at Jarvis for taking over the only town she'd ever really known. Rage at the US government for their incompetence. If regular people had some warning... If they knew what space weather could do...

Maybe Melody would have prepared. Maybe they all would have.

She wiped at her face again, smearing tears and dirt across her cheeks. "How did we get here?"

Colt shrugged. "Drove through the forest, mostly. I've tried to head due south."

Doug snorted a laugh, but Melody couldn't shake her anger and hopelessness. Larkin wouldn't even be able to cheer her up now. The thought of him sent another pang of heartache lancing through her body. He would never find them now.

"What are we going to do?"

Colt leaned forward and stared up at the still-dark sky. "Walk, I suppose. We can load up as many weapons as we can carry and bury the rest. Then we'll head southeast. We should hit Lake Tahoe sooner or later. Maybe one of the small towns Harvey talked about in between."

Melody glanced at her brother. "How far is it to Lake Tahoe?"

He scratched his head. "At least a hundred miles."

"A hundred miles!" The matte-painted metal of the military vehicle closed in around her and Melody struggled to breathe. "We're planning to walk a hundred miles to get to some lake we've never been to in the hopes there will be *something* there for us?"

Her brother turned sheepish. "When you put it like that…"

"What are we supposed to eat or drink on the way?"

No one said anything for a moment. At last, Dani broke the silence. "Do you have a better idea?"

Melody blinked. "Do you?"

"No. That's why I'm asking. Since you're so upset about the plan, is there something else you'd rather do?"

Melody sagged against the seat. She wished she could say yes, but every option she could think of wasn't any better. "No."

"Then stop complaining." Dani waited until Melody met her heavy gaze. "The situation sucks, we all know it. But I'm not giving up."

"Neither am I." Colt flashed a tight smile in agreement.

Melody wished she could share in their optimism, but all she could think about were the negatives. No food, no water, no shelter. Her neighbors were dead. Larkin was gone. How could they hike a hundred miles and not die on the way?

She asked another question. "How will we know which way to go?"

"I can land nav. Between the sun and the stars, we can head in the general direction." Colt scratched at his head. "From what I remember, Tahoe's huge. We won't miss it."

"You really think that's the best option?"

He nodded. "For right now, yes."

Melody thought about Larkin out there on his own, no idea how to find them in the miles of forest. She thought about all the what-ifs and the hope he'd given her.

"He'll find us."

She cut Colt a glance. "Easy for you to say."

Lottie squirmed, sticking her nose out to sniff at

Harvey's body. Melody pulled her back. "We need to bury Harvey and say a few words." Melody paused to maintain composure. "We might have left Gloria and Will out to the elements, but I won't do that to Harvey, too. He deserves a burial. They all deserve a memorial. To be remembered."

She didn't wait for anyone to respond. Grabbing the door handle, Melody jerked with all her might. The door opened and the cold morning air whipped her face.

* * *

It took Doug and Colt an hour to dig a deep enough grave with the shovel and pick axe stored underneath of the Humvee. The pair of them dragged Harvey into the ditch and Melody straightened his clothes before Doug filled the hole.

Melody stood at the makeshift cross Colt had fashioned out of a branch and closed her eyes. She tried to think of the right words to say. Something full of meaning and purpose that would do justice to the Wilkins family.

She opened her eyes. "I'm sorry, Harvey. I'm sorry for all of the mistakes of the past month. All the missed opportunities and sacrifices. All the hesitation and doubt. I'm sorry we failed your wife and grandson. Most of all, I'm sorry you died like this, running from strangers after the whole world turned upside down."

Doug reached out and squeezed her shoulder. There wasn't anything else Melody could say. What was the point of sharing her memories of a family that would soon live on only inside the minds of a handful of people?

Colt cleared his throat. "I owe Harvey Wilkins my life. If it weren't for his choice to pull me into his basement, I would be dead. Dani, too." He glanced at her and nodded. "Harvey gave up his own safety for a stranger and I will never forget that generosity."

Part of Melody wanted to scream. Beat her fists against Colt's chest and blame him for everything that happened. But what good would it do? What good would anything do?

It was only a matter of time before they all died. They were fooling themselves if they thought Lake Tahoe was a reality. She thrust Lottie into her brother's arms before walking away from the grave.

"Melody? Where are you going?"

She answered her brother without turning around. "I need a few minutes alone." Melody knew now how hopeless this powerless future would be. This moment, standing around with two strangers and the only family she had left in the world was the best it would ever get.

Her hair clung to her scalp in ratty, greasy clumps. Her jeans were stained with dirt and grime and a dead man's blood. She didn't know if the ring of black beneath her nails was filth or a permanent stain, but it didn't matter.

The old Melody Harper who loved to curl up on a couch and watch Hallmark Chanel movies with a pint of ice cream was dead. The animals she cared for at the vet clinic. All dead.

Just like her parents. Just like the Wilkinses.

Larkin was never coming back. No man would ever look at her and see the future again. Maybe a quick romp on a dirty floor or the leaf-strewn forest. But a wife? The mother of someone's children? Forget it. All the dreams she thought would still come true. All the things she'd hadn't crossed off her list.

Gone in the blink of an eye.

Maybe the power going out was punishment. Was this comeuppance for a world of frivolity and leisure? Was this some twisted retribution?

Melody walked without seeing. She didn't know where she was going. She planted her feet one after the other in the lumpy, dank earth. Thoughts of life and death and the meaning of it all swirled inside her head, more real than the forest all around.

She stumbled over a hidden log on the forest floor. The ground rose up, full of branches and leaves and broken twigs. Melody thrust her arms out to break her fall, only there wasn't any more ground. Her hands led the way as she tumbled off a hidden ledge.

As her body hit the first outcrop of rocks, her ribs crunched and splintered and Melody screamed.

CHAPTER TWENTY-THREE

DANI

Northern California Forest
    3:00 p.m.

Dani bent over and sucked in a lungful of air.
They had been searching for Melody for hours. At some
point, they had to accept reality. She stood up and
unscrewed the cap on one of the few bottles of water
they managed to salvage from the truck. A splash of
water hit her cracked lips.

Crap. She shoved the empty bottle in the back of the
Humvee and groaned. Spending their precious energy
circling out in wider and wider arcs around the Humvee
to search for Melody wasn't getting them anywhere.
They could all end up dead before too long.

As if he'd read her thoughts, Doug called out.
"We're not giving up. I can't leave without my sister."

Sometime over the last six hours, Doug aged a

decade. Gone were his wide-open eyes and easy smile. In their place, a haggard, broken man who couldn't admit what Colt and Dani already grasped: Melody was dead or dying.

Lottie yipped at Doug's feet and he scooped the hungry little dog up. "I know you miss her, Lot. I do, too." He ruffled her fur. "We'll find her. I promise."

He set Lottie down, but the little dog only pawed at his leg.

Dani stated the obvious. "She's hungry."

Doug cut her a glance. "We're all hungry."

"Someone needs to look for water and food. We've got a million guns, we should be able to shoot something."

"I'm not doing anything except search for my sister."

"You'd rather die out here, then? Because that's what'll happen if we don't find something to eat."

"Enough." Colt broke through a thicket of scrub brush and entered the small clearing where Doug and Dani stood. "Arguing will get us nowhere."

He set his rifle on the ground and stretched, wincing as his back bent. Dani didn't know how the man even managed to stay upright after the crash he survived. "Dani, how about you go on a hunt for water? There's got to be a stream or river nearby. They snake all through this area."

"What about Melody?"

Colt turned to Doug. "You and I can keep searching. We'll increase the radius, fan out from here and look for any signs of her."

"She could be miles away by now." *Or dead*, but

Dani didn't offer the most logical answer. Melody wasn't cut out for a hike in the forest. Without food or water, and no concept of direction, she didn't stand a chance. Even if she were only lost, the chances of finding her now, after searching for hours, had to be slim.

First Gran, then Gloria and Will, Harvey, and most likely Melody, too. At some point over the course of the night before, Dani turned it all off. Her emotions, hope, any thought or feeling that wasn't tied to her own base need to survive. Dani was ready to call off the search right now and hit the road.

She wasn't going to die out in the middle of the California forest searching for a needle in a haystack. Glancing up at the sun, she thought it over. If they weren't any closer to finding Melody by sunset, that was it. Dani would stay the night with Colt and Doug, but she would hightail it out of there first thing in the morning.

At some point those men from the road would come looking for them and she planned to be miles away by the time they found the Humvee. She headed over to the vehicle and dragged two empty jugs from the back.

"If I find water, I'll clean these out and fill them up."

"Good. Head for lower ground. You might find a stream tucked between two ridges, or a small fall on the slope of one of these hills." Colt picked up his rifle and motioned to a nearby tree. "Mark your path so you can get back. A notch on a tree every fifty steps."

"I can do that."

"Good." Colt turned to Doug. "Let's restart the

search. We've got three solid hours of daylight left. Let's make the most of it."

Dani watched the pair of them head out with Lottie trailing behind. The poor little dog would go the way of her owner if Dani didn't come back with at least something to drink. She grabbed a strip of rope from the Humvee and tied the jugs together before looping them over her shoulder along with a rifle.

As she traipsed through the underbrush, her worn-out sneakers slipped and skidded. The jugs banged against each other in a hollow echo and Dani slowed down. She couldn't listen for gurgling water if she couldn't hear anything but her own clumsy movements.

On and on she walked, slow enough to catch the sound of birds as they landed in the treetops above and squirrels jumping from one branch to the next. If she were a better shot, she might be able to kill one or two for a makeshift dinner.

Squirrel couldn't be any worse than the mystery meat from her old school cafeteria. They had more than enough ammo now; maybe it would be worth a try. She unslung the rifle from her shoulder and positioned the jugs so they stopped colliding as she moved.

With slow steps, she eased forward, looking and listening for an animal to kill. Hunting had never been her thing, but desperate times called for desperate measures. Dani was done running and hiding and hoping to survive by being invisible. She would own every decision from here on out.

She would live by choice, not by default.

The sound of rustling leaves stopped Dani mid-step.

She twisted in place. A deer stood no more than twenty feet away, ears pricked as it spotted her.

Dani eased into position. If she shot it, they would have meat for days. Saliva pooled in her mouth and she swallowed. As she stepped back into a crouch, a twig snapped. The deer spooked and ran. *Crap!* Dani hustled after it, skidding and slipping down a muddy embankment.

I can't lose it!

Her shoes squelched in the mud and Dani almost fell time and again. The jugs banged together on her back in a staccato drumbeat and sweat beaded along her brow. She couldn't slow down. She would catch the animal and bring something to the table.

The deer crashed through brush and Dani caught glimpses of its black tail in the dappled afternoon sun. *Come on. Just give me a clear shot.* With the rifle pinned to her shoulder, Dani ran as fast as possible, dodging leaves and branches, but the deer always stayed just out of range.

She couldn't catch it. Dani slowed, huffing and puffing out her exhaustion as the gap between her and the deer increased. A minute later, she lost sight of it in the trees.

Dani stopped. Blood thundered in her ears like a thousand tiny hooves. She sucked in one breath after another, panting as she leaned against the nearest tree. All that work for nothing.

She expended a ton of energy and what did it get

her? More hunger and thirst and a longer trek back to Colt.

After a few minutes, her breathing slowed and Dani looked around her. While chasing the deer, she'd skidded down a gentle slope. The pine trees of the roadside gave way to the big leafy varieties with branches that blocked out the fading sun.

She stopped to listen. Beneath the racing of her heart and the twittering of random birds, a constant rumble lurked. It couldn't be a train or a highway or a distant airport. Those things were long gone. No, it had to be a river.

But what direction?

Dani closed her eyes. The sound bounced off the higher grades of land, echoing on all sides. She turned in a slow circle, trying to place the source. She couldn't be sure, but her best guess was the path the deer had taken.

She glanced back the way she had come. How long had she run? Would she be able to find her way back?

Dani marked a tree where she stood with a double notch to remind her of where she stopped. It might not be enough, but what choice did she have? She couldn't backtrack now when the promise of a river lay out of sight.

Setting off in the direction of the deer, Dani kept one eye on the setting sun. If she stayed out much longer, she wouldn't make it back to the Humvee before dark. Hiking in the pitch black of night wasn't a welcome thought.

Dani picked up the pace, stopping every now and then to mark a tree or bend a branch. As she stepped through a tangled bramble, the ground dipped and she stumbled. The jugs clattered on her back, the rifle slipped off her shoulder, and Dani scrambled to grab the nearest tree.

Her hand slipped on the sapling, but she dug her nails into a branch, clinging on as her feet slipped out from under her. Leaves tore from the branch as she slid another foot. A ravine. Her feet dangled off the edge of a steep drop and the sound of a river rushed up from below.

Water.

With one hand still holding onto the tree and one thrust into the dirt for purchase, Dani eased to sit on the soft ledge. If she used her backside as an anchor and the trees as checks, she could make it to the bottom. Climbing up would be a massive undertaking.

She glanced up at the sky. Making it back before dark would be impossible. If she wanted to reach the river, she would need to camp there all night. Dani chewed on her lip. Could she do that? Could she figure out a way to survive at the edge of a rushing stream all alone?

Her parched lips cracked with her answer. She didn't have a choice. Water was the difference between life and death. Dani reached for the next tree and slid three feet down the hill. Gravel and sticks and pinecones rumbled past her. She reached for another tree.

Foot by foot, she made her agonizing descent toward the river. The rushing water grew louder and louder and the sun dipped lower as she trekked. At last, her feet landed hard on the bank and Dani laughed out loud.

Eight feet wide and crystal clear, the stream beckoned. Dani dumped her gear on the ground and rushed up to the water. Falling to her knees on the sandy shore, she scooped up the precious liquid in her hands and drank and drank until she couldn't swallow another drop.

Only when she reached her fill, did she lean back.

Oh, no. It can't be.

Ten yards downstream, a body floated half in the water. The other half lay tangled and broken among a fallen tree.

Dark hair, gray sweater, muddy jeans.

Dani stood up on shaky legs and made her way over. She reached down and pulled a clump of leaves and hair away from the woman's face. Melody's eyes, now gray and filmy, stared back in death.

CHAPTER TWENTY-FOUR

COLT

Northern California Forest
6:00 p.m.

"We need to get back. Dani will be waiting for us."

Doug tramped on ahead. "I have to find Melody."

Colt cursed under his breath. This entire expedition had gone to hell in a handbasket. "You need to accept reality, Doug."

"She's out here somewhere. Hurt or in trouble. I *will* find her."

Doug kept walking. With no plan and no destination in mind, he'd been circling the Humvee and growing more and more agitated as the minutes ticked by.

"We need to regroup and set up camp. I'm not saying we leave."

"Good, because that isn't an option."

Colt stopped in his tracks. "Damn it, Doug. We need a plan. I can't keep following you as you circle the drain."

Doug spun around to face Colt, fury and fear in his eyes. "I'm not giving up on her. She's the only family I have left. Melody means everything to me."

Colt inhaled. They must have bushwhacked through five miles of forest, maybe more, with no sign of Melody. Colt could get them back to the Humvee, but it would be a hell of a lot harder in the dark.

He appealed to the man's common sense. "As soon as the sun sets, we'll be blind out here. How can we help your sister if we get hurt ourselves?"

Doug refused to listen. "I won't stop looking." He spun back around and charged through the next clump of trees. "Melody! Mel, can you hear me?! Melody!"

Without water or food, exhaustion would take Doug faster than it took Colt. It had been years since he'd roughed it out in the field, but the memory of combat still lingered in his blood. He could survive worse conditions than this, but a civilian wasn't as hardy.

Even a firefighter had limits.

He checked the safety on his rifle for the thousandth time and followed Doug deeper into the woods.

"Melody! Melody!" Doug cupped his hands around his mouth and shouted until he grew hoarse.

"Down here!"

Doug whipped around. "I'm coming, Mel!"

Colt hesitated. That wasn't Melody's voice. It wasn't deep enough or filled with enough fear.

"Find the river!"

Shit. It was Dani. If she were hollering for help, then something happened. Colt hustled after Doug. The younger man busted through trees and slipped down the embankment like a bull finally freed from a pen. Branches snapped. Rocks tumbled.

Doug slid ten feet at a time, but it didn't stop him. Colt couldn't keep up. Between the concussion and the bruises, he would never make it down the ravine that fast. He refused to break an ankle because Doug lost his mind. He lost sight of the man halfway down the ravine.

It didn't take long to find him once Colt hit the ground.

Dani stood on the edge of the water, rifle pointing at a space between her feet and Doug's bent-over body. He kneeled in the sand, arms outstretched. A woman lay on the bank of the river, wet hair tangled around her head like a crown.

Melody.

From the looks of her, she'd been dead for hours. Doug hauled her stiff and lifeless body against his chest, sobbing as he pushed the hair from her gray cheeks. "No. Not you. Not you."

He cradled his dead sister, rocking her back and forth as he stared at her open, sightless eyes. Colt glanced at Dani, a question in the tilt of his brow.

She shook her head.

Just what he thought. Melody was dead when Dani found her. It made sense. From the way the body lay stiff and bent, with her neck twisted at an impossible angle, it was obvious what happened.

Melody took a wrong turn and fell down the side of the hill. She died before she ever hit the ground.

Colt peered through the trees. They had maybe twenty minutes of decent light left. He turned back to Doug. "I'm sorry, Doug."

Doug snapped his head up and pointed a shaky, accusatory finger at Dani. "She did this."

"What? No!" Dani's mouth fell open as her gaze shifted between Doug and Colt. "I found her like that."

"Liar! You pushed her. I know it!" Doug dropped his sister on the bank. Her arm splashed in the water as he rushed to stand. His nostrils flared as he took a step toward Dani.

Colt held up a hand. "That's enough, Doug. She's told you the truth. Back off."

"She's lying." Doug's eyes stayed trained on Dani. "You've always been jealous of my sister. What, did you see her wandering in the forest and push her? Did she ask for your help before you sent her to her death?"

Dani clamped her mouth shut and her lips thinned to a line.

"So you don't deny it. I knew it!" Doug took another step.

Colt pulled his Sig from the holster. "I told you, not another step."

Doug's eyes flashed to Colt. "Did you tell her to do it?"

Colt sighted the center of Doug's chest. "Don't be ridiculous. I've risked my life to save you and Melody. Why would I want her dead?"

"Maybe this was your plan all along. Get us all out

here. Pick us off one by one. For all I know you staged the accident." Doug took a step toward Colt. "Tell me, did you know those men in the Mustang? Are they part of your crew?"

Was it the dehydration, hunger, or grief that concocted these crazy theories? Maybe all three. Colt exhaled. Doug wouldn't rile him up. "You're exhausted and starving, Doug. You're not thinking straight."

"Oh, I disagree. In fact, I think I'm finally seeing clearly." He took another step and a smile tipped his lips. "What are you going to do, shoot me?"

"If I have to. How about we just take a step back and relax? We can hike back to the Humvee while there's some light left, get some sleep, and discuss this like adults in the morning."

Dani interrupted. "I don't think—"

Doug turned on her. "That's right. You never think about anyone but yourself. This whole mess wouldn't have happened if you never showed up at Harvey's place. If the asshole hadn't taken you in and felt sorry for you, my sister would still be alive. We would still be sitting in our parents' house, comfortable and happy."

He twisted back and looked at his sister's body. "Melody would still be alive."

As Doug stared at his sister's body, Lottie burst through the brush at the river's edge. She scampered up to Melody, yipping and barking. Leaves and twigs matted the poor dog's fur as she sat at her dead master's side.

Colt swallowed. Everything had gone so horribly wrong. He cared for Melody. Hell, he could have fallen for her if the situation were different. And now she was dead and her brother was falling apart.

He lowered the gun and stepped forward. "Let's go back, Doug. We can carry Melody together and find a beautiful spot to bury her."

Doug screamed in anguish. Lottie cowered, but she wouldn't leave Melody's side. Doug rushed toward the little dog, hands outstretched like talons.

Dani shouted out. "If you touch that dog, you're a dead man."

Doug kept walking. "You don't have the balls."

Dani aimed and fired at a spot three feet to Doug's left. "Wanna bet?"

Shit. Colt didn't know how to diffuse the situation. Doug wasn't thinking clearly and Dani wasn't about to back down. As Colt stood there, gun still aimed at Doug, the grieving man spun around.

He unslung his rifle and pointed it at Dani, but his grip was all wrong. Even if Doug got a shot off, the kick would send him backward into the river. He'd end up on his ass before he could shoot again.

Colt spoke slowly and without emotion. "Don't do this, Doug. You don't want to die today."

"Don't I? What's the point now? Melody's dead. Harvey and Gloria and Will are dead. Larkin is God knows where." He waved the rifle around, finger too tight on the trigger. "We're going to die out here anyway, might as well get it over with."

"You're in shock. Hand me the rifle and we can talk about it in the morning."

Doug swung the gun back to Dani. "No. She deserves to be punished."

Colt had to give Dani credit. She stood still, aiming at Doug's chest, saying nothing. The barrel of the rifle didn't even shake. The girl might make it in this new world after all.

As they all stood there in a stalemate, Lottie let out a single, high-pitched bark. Doug turned.

It was Colt's chance. If he wanted to take the man out, now was the time. He took aim. His finger slipped around the trigger as Larkin burst through the trees.

"Well I'll be damned. If it isn't...oh, shit." He stumbled to a stop at the sight of Melody's corpse.

Doug spun around and pointed his rifle at Larkin. "Stand back!"

Larkin lifted his hands. "I don't know what's going on, but you need to lower your weapon."

"Were you in on it?"

"In on what?" Larkin glanced at Colt as another figure emerged from the trees.

Colt blinked in surprise. A man in his mid-forties with a two-inch beard came to a stop next to Larkin, his blue eyes clear and calm. *It can't be.*

"Walter Sloane? Is that you?"

CHAPTER TWENTY-FIVE

COLT

NORTHERN CALIFORNIA FOREST
7:00 p.m.

WALTER SLOANE. THE PILOT WHO LANDED A commercial jet on a tiny runway after the power went out. The first man to save Colt's life post-EMP. What the hell was he doing in the middle of the Northern California forest?

He looked a little older, maybe a little more haggard, but otherwise the man appeared in excellent health. A beard coated his previously clean jaw and out of the pilot's uniform he seemed a bit younger, but it was definitely the same man.

Colt nodded in his direction. "Good to see you again, Pilot. Wish the circumstances were better."

Walter nodded, but didn't say anything. Colt tried to take in the scene from Walter's perspective. An air marshal and a teenage girl pointing weapons at a distraught man standing over the corpse of a woman. Not exactly the warmest welcome.

Larkin stared at Melody's dead body where it lay on the creek's edge. Colt could see the emotion working behind the man's clenched jaw. After a moment, Larkin glanced up at Doug. "Is there a problem?"

"Are you blind? Melody's dead!" Doug jerked his rifle in Dani's direction. "And it's all her fault!"

Larkin managed to keep his voice even. "Is that right?"

"No." Dani shook her head while she held the rifle. "I found her in the river. She was already dead."

"The ravine is almost hidden in the tree line." Colt tilted his head toward the embankment. "Melody must have fallen."

Doug trembled. "No way. Melody wouldn't be so careless."

Colt pressed on. "She was distraught. Harvey's death wrecked her. Don't you remember, Doug? She could barely stand at his grave."

The rifle in Doug's hands shook. "I don't believe it."

Colt tried again. "It would have been easy to catch a rock or break a leg. I slid a bunch of times."

"Better you than her."

"That's enough, Doug." Larkin eased forward again. "Dani told you what happened. Let it go."

"I won't."

Colt watched Larkin. He couldn't get a read on his old friend. How much had he shared with Melody? Had their relationship changed into something more? As

Larkin stepped toward Doug, Colt prepared to shoot anyone who made a wrong move.

Larkin pulled a pistol from his waistband and held it close to his chest. He reached out with his other hand to Doug. "Hand me the weapon."

"No." Doug swung the rifle in Larkin's direction. "It's mine."

Larkin didn't even flinch. "If I remember correctly, it actually belongs to that asshole who killed the Wilkins family."

Doug stared at the dark metal barrel for a moment. It was enough for Larkin. He lunged for the gun and plucked it from Doug's hands before he had time to react.

Doug stood there, hands still in the shape of the rifle, frozen.

Larkin turned to Walter. "Does your offer still stand?"

Walter glanced at Colt. "Yes. But the first sign of trouble and you all will have to leave. Understood?"

Colt didn't know what the hell was going on, but if Walter was offering, he was taking, whatever it might turn out to be. He nodded at Walter before turning his attention on Doug. The man needed to come to terms with reality. Colt holstered his weapon and approached.

"We can all help with Melody, if that's what you want."

Doug shuddered while he stared at his sister's corpse. "No. She's my responsibility. I can bury her."

Colt exhaled. He didn't want to push, but leave Doug there to handle his sister on his own? He stepped back to stand beside Dani and motioned for her to stand down. She lowered the rifle with a scowl.

Larkin bent down and scooped Lottie up into his arms. "Walter has some food. I'm going to get Lottie something to eat. Is that all right, Doug?"

Melody's brother swayed back and forth on his feet, never once taking his eyes off her body. "Fine."

Larkin motioned to Walter and the pair of them eased around Doug and joined Colt and Dani on the bank. Walter gave Colt's hand a quick shake. "Looks like you all are in a bind."

Colt nodded. "That's an understatement."

"I've got a base camp not far from here. You are welcome to come rest there."

"We've got a Humvee up the hill with some gear and quite a few weapons."

Walter nodded. "We can collect everything tomorrow. How about all of you come with me before it's too dark to see?"

Colt glanced up at the sky. Sometime during the altercation with Doug, the sun had set. They didn't have long. "Thank you, but someone should stay with Doug."

"No. I want to be alone."

Colt knew the man's grief was eating him up, but he couldn't leave Doug to the elements. "What will you do overnight?"

"Bury my sister."

Larkin caught Colt's eye. "I'll come back to check on him in a while."

Leaving Doug didn't sit well with Colt, but what choice did he have? If he stayed, it would only prolong the conflict. If he left, Doug could mourn his sister in peace. Both options were terrible, but with reluctance, Colt agreed. "I'll be back at first light."

Doug didn't respond. He walked over to his sister's body and knelt by her side. Colt turned away. Doug needed time to grieve without a bunch of people he barely knew staring at him, wondering if he would crack.

Walter pointed downriver and Colt, Dani, and Larkin fell into step behind him. Lottie sat in the crook of Larkin's arm, her little ears pricked as she listened to the evening animals of the forest waking up. The poor little scrap of a dog had been through more than most pets, and now her owner was dead.

Colt didn't know how long an animal like Lottie would last in this new world, but he would try his best to keep her alive for Melody's sake.

With a heaviness in his heart, he left the woman he'd grown attached to in unexpected ways behind. So far, the trek out of Eugene had brought nothing but pain and misfortune. He hoped Walter's presence would turn the tide.

CHAPTER TWENTY-SIX

COLT

Northern California Forest
9:00 p.m.

Colt swirled the last dregs of tea around his mug and gulped it down. "I can't thank you enough for letting us come here."

Walter nodded. "You're welcome. I could frankly do with some company. It's been a long week on my own."

Larkin, Walter, Colt, and Dani sat in a circle around a small fire, watching the flames dance. They'd been mostly silent for the past hour, drinking tea, eating some of Walter's jerky, and recovering from one hell of a day.

Colt reached out with a stick and poked a log not yet burning into the fire. "So you've been out here hunting?"

"Gathering anything I can find, really. Meat, edible

plants, berries. If it's not poisonous and I can preserve it, that's what I aim to do."

Colt stretched out his left leg and rubbed at the healed knife wound in his thigh. He had bruises all over from the car crash, injuries from the last month that weren't completely healed, and a concussion that still made him close his eyes every now and then. Walter on the other hand, seemed right as rain.

For a man who set off with nothing but a pilot's uniform and a couple of granola bars, he'd done a hell of a lot better than Colt expected. With a stretch and a groan, Colt eased a loaded question across the night. "So… where are you located these days?"

Walter smiled over the rim of his mug. "Not going to tell you that."

"Fair enough." Colt glanced at Larkin and exhaled. He didn't expect the truth from Walter, even if he'd gotten an answer. They might have both survived the same emergency landing, but Walter didn't know Colt from a hole in the ground. "Tell me about Sacramento. It had to fare worse than Eugene."

Walter filled him in on the details, describing everything from the looting and fires to the National Guard sealing up the worst riots and letting them burn themselves out. It sounded like he barely escaped the violence. Walter poked a stick at the fire keeping them warm. "What about Eugene? When I went through, it was fine. Why leave?"

Colt shared his experience staying at the University of Oregon for the first two weeks and how the National Guard who came to help went rogue. He told Walter all about Jarvis and the night he barely escaped with his life and how Dani kept him alive, and how Harvey took them in when they were on death's door.

Larkin chimed in with what he experienced in Portland and then how the National Guard turned into a militia.

At the end of it all, Walter nodded. "If there's anything I've learned this past month, it's that finding people to trust is worth more than any skill."

Colt agreed. He didn't know which one fared worse: the big city with complete lawlessness, or the small town with a despot for a ruler. But the conversation with Walter solidified his decision to find a remote place on his own.

Nowhere bigger than a few thousand people would be functional now. Small towns with tight-knit communities might be able to carry on with some semblance of normalcy, but without the government as de facto leaders, the power loss would warp everywhere eventually.

He thought about all of his assignments halfway across the world and the tribal factions that mattered more than any dictator or president. America was in the throes of a crisis and in desperate times—not always the best men and women took charge.

While Walter poured another cup of tea, Colt took stock. A single tent for one in forest green sat concealed among the trees on the edge of the camp. Sacks of gathered food sat beside the entrance.

A crazy box with aluminum foil sides and a clear plastic lid took up residence not far from the fire. Colt squinted at it. Was it a storage container? A magnifying glass? All of a sudden it clicked. A solar cooker. *Smart*.

The fire in the middle was one of two. Another, larger version with rocks and sheets of metal anchored the opposite corner of the camp. A deer carcass hung above it, high enough to avoid animals attracted by the smell as it smoked.

Colt pointed at the setup. "Are you cooking all of that meat?"

Walter glanced behind him. "Hoping to smoke it, actually. It won't keep unless I preserve it somehow. I wanted to can it, but the logistics were too hard. I made jerky out of the last one, but I wanted to try my hand at something different this go-round."

The difference between their situations was staggering. In town, they were rummaging through houses and fending off hostiles and barely surviving. Out in the woods, Walter had abundance and plenty.

Colt glanced at Dani. She sat a few feet away, toes pointed toward the fire while Lottie slept in her lap. She chewed on a strip of deer jerky in silence, watching the flames.

The little dog had gorged herself on scraps of the hanging deer while Walter had stoked the fire and put the water on to boil. If Colt didn't have the wounds to prove it, he could almost forget the rest of the country was falling apart.

He nudged Dani's foot with his boot. "You can curl up somewhere and sleep."

She raised her exhausted head. "Where?"

Walter pointed at a large leafy tree among the pines.

"There's a soft spot beneath the white alder over there. You'll be close enough to the smoker that you shouldn't be cold."

Dani glanced at it, but didn't move.

Colt nudged her again. "I'll wake you if anything happens."

"You promise?"

He nodded and Dani reluctantly stood, carrying her rifle with her over to the tree. She patted the ground around the trunk and eased herself down. Lottie trotted up and tucked herself by Dani's side.

Colt waited for a handful of minutes before turning back to Walter. He needed to clear the air. "I'm sorry again about the scene with Doug. We only beat you to the river by a few minutes."

"Larkin told me you'd already lost two people."

"Three." Colt glanced at Larkin. The man had been quiet for the better part of the night. "Harvey's dead, too."

"Damn it." Larkin scrubbed a hand down his face. "It wasn't supposed to go like this."

Colt agreed. Ever since they left Eugene, their luck had taken a turn for the worse. "I'm sorry about Melody."

"Are you sure she fell?"

"As sure as I can be. For one, I believe Dani. For another, Melody's neck was broken, leaves and twigs were all tangled in her hair, and her jeans were covered in mud. I'm not a detective, but it sure as hell looked like an accident."

Larkin nodded and stood up. "I'm going to check on Doug."

"Are you sure?"

He paused as a shadow crossed his face. "I also want to pay my respects."

Colt nodded. "See you in the morning."

Larkin slung a rifle over his shoulder and took off.

After his footsteps faded into the night, Colt turned to Walter. "How did you and Larkin find each other?"

"I came across him near Highway 58. Told me he'd been chased by a pair of men up to no good and was trying to find his way back to his group. I offered to help. We were on our way to this place when we came across you all."

Colt snorted. They only ran into each other on accident. Maybe their luck hadn't completely run out.

"How did you end up with the girl? Was she on the plane?"

"No." Colt leaned back and took another sip of tea. "I found her on the streets in Eugene. She'd been caught by a soldier who wanted to bring her in. He didn't have good intentions, so I rectified the situation."

"And you two have stuck together ever since?"

"She's saved my life and I've saved hers." Colt glanced at Dani's sleeping form. "Guess she's the closest to family I'm ever going to get."

Walter nodded. "In times like these, family is what matters."

"How about you? Did you find your wife and daughter?"

Walter didn't answer. Instead he sipped his tea. After

a moment, he changed the subject. "Tell me about the gun haul. Larkin described the car crash and two men in the Mustang. I want your take on it."

Colt relayed what he knew. When he finished, he asked the question that burned in the back of his mind ever since overhearing the two men talk. "Do you know anything about this Cunningham fellow?"

"If it's the man I'm thinking of, he can't be trusted." Walter stared past the glow of the small fire at their feet and into the darkness. "He's more of a cult leader than anything else. One of those end times types."

Not the answer Colt hoped to hear. "What else do you know?"

"Not much. We've tried to keep clear."

We. That meant Walter wasn't alone. Colt figured as much, but confirmation was good. Maybe Walter would be willing to take them in for a time. At least until they could regroup and determine where to go. He tossed out a feeler. "Our group plans to head to Lake Tahoe."

"I wouldn't. It's overrun with people from Reno and Sacramento. Everyone flocked to it when they fled the cities."

Damn. "Then where do you suggest?"

"Somewhere small with access to running water. A place that you can secure without constant patrols and can keep you alive through the winter. We'll have a cool, comfortable summer in these parts, but winter comes in hard and quick if you aren't ready for it."

Colt snorted. Nowhere like that existed without planning. "So fairytale land, that's what you're saying."

"You just have to take your time and look."

"I'm not sure time is on our side."

"Then I guess you'll have to work a bit—"

Larkin burst into the clearing as Walter spoke. His face was flushed with exertion, but his eyes held nothing but pain and dread. Whatever he had to say, it wasn't good.

DAY THIRTY-FOUR

CHAPTER TWENTY-SEVEN

DANI

Northern California Forest

7:00 a.m.

Dani sat up and rubbed the sleep from her eyes. Despite passing out on the forest floor, she actually felt halfway decent. It had been the first night since Colt regained consciousness at Harvey's place that she didn't wake up every hour.

Exhaustion had its merits. She brushed the dirt and leaves off her jeans and headed out into the woods to find a secluded spot to relieve herself. It sure beat nasty toilets and city sewage.

She tramped back into the clearing as Walter emerged from his tent. Dani glanced around. The fire was out and Lottie still slept in the same spot she'd left her. She didn't bother to say hello. "Where are Colt and Larkin?"

Walter glanced up as he zipped the tent closed. "They left early this morning."

Dani frowned. It was unlike Colt to leave without telling her. "Is something wrong?"

Walter hesitated.

"If you don't tell me, I'm setting off to find them right now."

Walter exhaled. "You're a lot like my daughter. Strong-willed and impatient." He walked over to the fire and crouched in front of it. "Larkin left to check on your friend last night. When he came back, he said Doug was missing."

"What do you mean, missing?"

Walter shrugged. "That's all I know. Colt made the decision to sleep for a few hours. Said he wouldn't be any good on a night mission in his state. They took off as soon as it lightened up enough to see."

Dani shook her head. "He should have told me. I could help."

"Colt would like you to stay."

Dani threw her hands in the air. "That's ridiculous. Three sets of eyes are better than two."

"I'm sure between an army officer and a former SEAL, they can find one city firefighter in the woods."

"How would you know?"

"Marine Corps, retired."

Dani frowned. She hated the thought of Colt out there without her, but Walter had a point. Larkin would be a better sidekick than she could ever be. But it didn't mean she wanted to be left behind. What if they ran into trouble?

So many questions swirled around in her head. So many conflicting emotions. She didn't know the man crouched in front of the fire. He seemed like a good guy, but even her mom could clean up nice. Dani had half-listened to the men talk about how they met and their experiences over the last month, but she'd been so tired, she missed plenty.

Part of her wanted to stay like Colt asked and part of her wanted to rush out and find him. She chewed on a nail. "So you have a daughter?"

Walter nodded. "She's a few years older than you. Almost finished her second year in college before the EMP."

"Are you a good father?"

The question caught Walter off guard and he blinked. "You don't mince words, do you?"

"What's the point? It's not like being polite will get me anything but dead."

"I suppose not." Walter flicked a lighter and held it to a dry bit of fluff. It caught on fire and he eased it under the half-burned logs from the night before. Only then did he answer. "I'd like to think of myself as a good dad, yeah. I love my daughter. I would do anything to protect her and keep her safe. Maybe I was a little hard on her when she was younger, but I hope she appreciates it now."

Dani swallowed. Walter sounded like the best dad ever. What she would have given for someone other than Gran to give a rip about her. She worked her lower lip back and forth between her teeth. "Where is she now? Why isn't she out here with you?"

He watched the flames of the fire rise as he answered. "When we left Sacramento, we headed up here to a cabin one of my daughter's friends knew about. It's safe and secure and Madison is with her mother. I'm here pulling my weight. I can't live off other people's generosity. I have to contribute."

Dani knew exactly how he felt. She tucked a strand of hair behind her ear. "Thank you for letting us stay here overnight."

"It sounded like you were in a desperate situation."

She pursed her lips. "I'm not giving up."

"I never said you were."

"The car crash wasn't our fault. We couldn't do anything to stop it."

"I didn't say it was."

"Colt and I will make it. We're survivors." Dani didn't know why she felt the need to defend herself to this stranger, but she couldn't help it. He needed to know she wasn't some helpless girl who needed saving. She would survive even if he turned his back on them.

Walter poked at the fire. "I've got some food if you're hungry. It's not bacon and eggs, but there's more jerky and I dried some early salmonberries I found the other day. There's even a patch of miner's lettuce closer to the creek."

Dani's mouth opened, but no sound came out. She swallowed and tried again. "I've already taken some of your food. I...I can go without."

"It's not a problem." He stood and made his way to a collection of sacks of various sizes before waving her over. "Come, I'll show you."

Walter pulled open a sack at his feet. He scooped a small cup into the sack and came out with some pink things that looked like lumpy raisins. "Salmonberries usually aren't ripe until May or June but this bush must have gotten a bunch of early sun." He held the cup out as Dani walked up. "I dried them a few days ago. Help yourself."

Dani plucked a single fruit. She sniffed it before taking a tentative bite. Sugar and tart exploded inside her mouth and she almost smiled. "It's kind of like a raspberry."

"Indeed." Walter closed the bag before reaching for another. "I've also harvested some burdock root. We can mash it up and fry it. Tastes sort of like a parsnip."

A parsnip. Dani racked her brain, but came up empty. "Is that a like a potato?"

Walter chuckled. "Let me guess, you grew up in the city."

Dani didn't know what to say so she shoved another dried berry in her mouth. She didn't want to tell the man that he might as well be speaking a foreign language.

Memories of Gloria teaching her how to shell peas sprang to mind and Dani's tongue turned to lead. She forced the berry down her throat and thumped her chest. "My mother wasn't real good with this sort of stuff."

"I'd be happy to teach you."

Dani focused on the ground. Why was he being so nice? Did he want something? Was he going to use her against Colt somehow? He couldn't be just a good guy with no ulterior motives. People like that didn't survive anymore. It didn't work for the Wilkins family or Melody… or maybe even Doug.

She kicked at a pinecone and watched it roll away. "Why are you being so nice to me?"

"Because the more I get to know you, the more hope I have for the future."

Dani glanced up. He didn't seem to be blowing smoke. The open look on his face said he meant every word. It didn't make sense. Why would anything she said give him hope? "I'm nothing special."

"That's exactly why I have hope. You're not standing there snarfing down my food, or complaining about the woods, or thinking only of what you've lost."

"I would never do that."

"Because you aren't looking for someone else to save you. You've decided to save yourself."

Dani supposed Walter was right. Was that the difference between her life before the EMP and now? Before the grid failed, was she spending her days secretly wishing for someone to swoop in and save her from her mom and the life she was forced to live?

She sucked in a deep breath and huffed it out. Maybe Walter was everything he said he was and more, but she wouldn't take his generosity lying down. She pointed at the sack. "Would you mind showing me what you've harvested? I need to know what's edible around here."

Walter smiled. "It would be my pleasure."

The two of them worked through every sack and

container Walter had assembled and then moved onto various plants around the campsite. Dani sampled everything from miner's lettuce to dandelion greens to young cattail shoots.

Walter explained what grew when and what to look for along the creek bed versus inside the forest. He even showed Dani how to make tea out of elderberry flowers and wild violets.

She smiled over the rim of her mug. "Thank you for everything. I never knew so much food grew in the middle of nowhere."

"Believe me, neither did I. If it weren't for some enterprising friends of my daughter, I wouldn't be much better off than you. I can hunt, but I always left the foraging to others."

Dani sipped her tea and nodded. For the first time in forever, hope blossomed in her chest. Even if they had to camp in the woods, with a little bit of knowledge, they could survive. She turned to reach for the pot of hot water when the mug in her hands shattered.

Ceramic shards flew in all directions. One jagged piece lanced her cheek and Dani screamed.

Walter grabbed her and dragged her to the ground. "Get to the rifles! Now!"

He shielded her with his body as they scrambled across the ground. Shots rang out from a position deep in the forest. Dani couldn't tell if it was one shooter or a whole militia full of men. Blood coated her cheek and oozed down her neck as bullets pocked the dirt at her feet.

Walter lunged for a rifle and tossed it back to her as she spun around. Whoever was shooting wouldn't kill her without a fight.

CHAPTER TWENTY-EIGHT

COLT

Northern California Forest
   7:00 a.m.

"Where the hell did he go?" Colt traipsed through the forest, an arm's length away from Larkin. The pair had been circling the muddy river bank where they found Melody's body for over an hour looking for any sign of her brother.

"Hell if I know."

"What did he do with Melody's body?" Colt couldn't make heads or tails of what must have happened in the night. When Larkin came back to Walter's camp explaining he couldn't find Doug, Colt blew it off. He figured the guy needed some time to grieve.

The last thing Colt wanted to do was confront Doug again in the dark. But now that they couldn't find a single trace of him, Colt second-guessed himself. Maybe if they'd gone straight back and hunted the surrounding area, they would have come across him and been able to calm the grieving man down.

"We've looked up and down the creek and he's not there. I didn't see any mound for a burial site, either." Larkin paused to think. "That means he either took her body back to the Humvee or he's gone completely crazy and run off with her into the forest."

Colt gulped a mouthful of water from the canteen Walter let him borrow and nodded. "Let's hit the Humvee. If he's there, great. If not, we can strip the Humvee and haul everything back to the camp."

"What do you know about Walter?"

"He saved an entire planeload of people when the power went out." Colt scratched at his beard. "Beyond that, not much. He left as soon as we landed. Said he had a wife and daughter in Sacramento he needed to get back to."

"Where are they?"

Colt shrugged. "Somewhere safe is my guess. You've seen his setup. He's obviously gathering food for more than just himself."

Larkin nodded. "I was so thankful when I ran into him yesterday, I didn't ask any questions. A man with venison jerky in his pocket is a good man to know."

Colt agreed. If all went well, running into Walter might mean the difference between living and merely hanging on. "I think we should offer him some of the guns and ammo. It's the least we can do."

"Sounds fair. It's not like we can carry them all anyway."

The pair of military men lapsed into silence as they hiked toward the Humvee. Colt kept his eyes open for any sign of Doug, but they reached the vehicle with no further clues as to the man's disappearance. Colt set his rifle down and leaned against the fender. "Let's strip this thing and then go dig up the weapons. We should be able to haul it all back if we use the cammie netting to make a sled."

After a few minutes of rest, Colt and Larkin set to work. Colt hauled the netting out of the rear of the vehicle and set the netting poles on top. Larkin popped the hood and pulled the easily accessible engine belts and the battery.

The inside yielded the pioneer kit Colt had already used to bury Harvey, the SINGCARS radio, and corresponding SL-3 kit. Colt thought back to the first night he regained consciousness at the Wilkins family home. Will had tuned in the radio to hear Walter's voice admonishing them to not give up hope.

He wondered if the man still had the ability to broadcast. If he didn't, he would by the time Colt lugged the radio back to camp.

Larkin stopped to stare at all the gear. "You find a pack mule in there, too?"

Colt chuckled. "I think you're lookin' at him."

"You find any whiskey in there?"

"Not a drop."

"Damn." Larkin shook his head. "That's priority number one when we find another town. Whiskey. I am not huffing all this stuff a hundred miles without a payoff at the end."

"I'm hoping we won't have to go nearly that far."

Larkin paused. "Walter's place?"

"Or somewhere nearby. It can't hurt to ask."

"I suppose not. But you know what is gonna hurt?"

"Carrying all this?"

"And the ammo, too. Don't forget the ammo."

Colt groaned. "Lead the way, soldier. I was too busy burying Harvey to know what you did with it."

Larkin motioned toward a makeshift path due south of the Humvee. He stopped at the base of a gnarled pine tree. The ground beneath the lower branches was fresh and free of debris. "It should all be here. Guns and ammo, both." He frowned. "I swear I covered it better than this, though."

With the shovel and the pick axe Colt and Larkin took turns digging up the loose soil above the guns. Colt struck something solid first. "I've hit something."

Larkin gave a start. "No way. I buried everything way deeper than that." He fell to his knees and used the pick axe's blunt side to scrape away the dirt. Instead of a black duffel bag, he exposed the graying flesh of a human arm. He leaned back in shock. "What the—?"

Colt kneeled beside him and together they uncovered enough of the body to confirm what neither expected: Melody. "Doug must have buried her here."

"But why?"

All the answers that he came to find filled Colt with dread. A few more than others. "The bags might still be beneath her. We need to move her."

Larkin stared at Melody's corpse for a moment before moving. "Right. Of course." He reached for her, sliding his hands beneath her ribs. As he stood up, the dirt fell away, exposing her dark brown curls and cold, dead skin.

Colt attacked the hole with the shovel, scooping and throwing dirt as quickly as possible. After five minutes of solid effort, he stopped. "They aren't here."

"Not a single one?"

"Doug took everything. The duffels. The ammo. All of it. I'm down to hard-packed earth."

Larkin's jaw tightened into a steel line. His muscles flexed as he lowered Melody back into the grave. "When we find him, I'm beating the answer out of him. I don't care if he was Melody's brother or not."

Larkin stalked off to ready the supplies while Colt re-buried Melody's body. By the time he finished, sweat soaked his shirt, but did nothing to dissipate his anger. Doug had been hard to read from the start. When they worked together to rescue Gloria from the militia, Colt thought the man had changed. But after this…

If they did find Doug, Colt wouldn't stop Larkin from doing what he promised. They couldn't risk anyone's safety with a man who might have gone off the rails.

Before he left, Colt paused at the edge of Melody's grave. He didn't have a cross or a bouquet of flowers, but he could say a few words. "I'm sorry for all that you suffered at the hands of Jarvis and Captain Ferguson and the militia. I never meant to mix you, your brother, or the Wilkins family up in any of it.

"You were nothing but kind to me. Hell, thanks to your handiwork with a needle I'm not oozing pus and trying to chop off my own leg." He knelt and put one hand on the middle of Melody's grave. "I'll miss you, Melody. I'm sorry you can't continue on this journey with us."

Colt walked back to the Humvee with a somber, heavy step. He found Larkin packed and ready. The former soldier leaned against the closed door and stared off into the distance. "Is it done?"

"Yes."

Larkin pushed off the door and reached for the sled he'd concocted out of the netting and poles. "Good. "Let's get back to Walter and Dani."

"Do you want to see it? Say anything?"

"No. Standing over her grave won't do anything but waste time."

"I'm sorry, Larkin."

"Me, too." He huffed one end of the pole up with a grimace. "Ready?"

Colt grabbed the other pole and exhaled. "As I'll ever be."

Together, the two of them dragged the heavy load back to Walter's camp, over rises and down slopes, around trees and through mud. By the time they reached the river, both men were exhausted. Colt set his side down and stopped to splash water over his face.

As Larkin bent to do the same, a shot rang out. Colt stood up with a start. "Dani."

Larkin pulled his rifle off his shoulder. "Let's go."

They were still a mile away. As they ran, more shots rang out, one after the other in a steady stream until the magazine emptied. Thirty seconds later, the shots began anew.

"We'll never make it. Whoever is shooting could fire a thousand rounds at Dani and Walter before we reach the camp."

Colt picked up the pace. "Then we have to hope like hell they've got somewhere to hide." As he ran toward the sound of round after round, Colt threw up a prayer.

If Dani and Walter could stay alive until they got there, Colt would put an end to it. Whoever was trying to kill them wouldn't make it out of that forest alive.

CHAPTER TWENTY-NINE

DANI

Northern California Forest
12:00 p.m.

Dani didn't know where to aim. The sound of the shots echoed through the forest and the rounds landing in the dirt weren't concentrated enough to matter. Walter dove behind a stack of firewood and Dani scrambled after him. She ducked as another round sailed over her head and lodged in the pine five feet away.

"Whoever's shooting is a terrible shot!" Walter pulled back the bolt action on his hunting rifle and turned toward the direction of the gunfire.

Only one person came to mind. "It's Doug."

"What?" Walter glanced at Dani like she'd gone mad. "He's part of your group."

"He blames me for Melody's death."

"You didn't do it, did you?"

Dani stomped her irritation down. "Of course not. I liked Melody. She was my friend."

"Then why is he shooting at you?"

"It's complicated."

Walter ducked as another round sailed past them. "I'm not going anywhere."

Dani twisted in place until she could prop the rifle on a log halfway up the stack. If Doug made an appearance, she would be ready. As she stared down the barrel, she answered Walter. "They were under the radar of the militia until we showed up. If Harvey hadn't taken me and Colt in and if Melody hadn't saved Colt's life, then they would all still be in Eugene."

"I see."

Dani cut Walter a glance. "They didn't have to take us in. They could have left Colt on the street to die."

"I suppose."

"Or they could have kicked us out when he recovered. They made the choice to stand by us."

"And suffer the consequences?"

"Whose side are you on?"

Walter shrugged. "No one's. But now I'm stuck in the crossfire."

"Then you need to choose." Dani concentrated on the forest. She was done talking to Walter. If he wanted to shoot her and wave the white flag of surrender, he could freakin' go ahead. But she wasn't taking her eyes off the tree line. Doug was out there somewhere and if Walter wasn't going to ruin her day, then she was going to take Doug down.

The gunfire paused and Dani took a chance. "What's the matter, Doug? Can't figure out how to reload?" She took off for the tent, ignoring Walter's shouts to stay hidden. As she dove behind the green nylon, another volley of fire rang out. It didn't matter. Dani wasn't going down like this. She wasn't letting a man stricken with grief put a bullet in her chest because he couldn't accept reality.

She ran in a crouch out from the tent and into the dense foliage of the forest. Branches scraped her face and roots threatened to trip her up, but Dani kept going. She needed to lure Doug away from Walter and out into the open.

A brave little bark sounded at her feet and Dani glanced down. Lottie's brown and gray fur streaked past her toward the direction of the rounds. "Lottie! No!"

Dani chased after the little dog. Lottie's speed increased the distance between them, but Dani followed the almost constant barking. As the sound grew louder, she slowed. Doug wouldn't shoot Melody's dog, would he?

Ducking behind a tree, Dani took stock. The land around her rose in a gentle incline and up to what appeared to be the crest of a hill. The river tracked down behind her, too far to hear. All she could see were trees and brambles and leaves everywhere. Ferns covered the ground and obscured all but the largest tree roots. Lottie would be lost a foot beneath the ground cover.

A bark sounded from up the hill. A shush followed

right behind. *Doug*. If she could hear him, he couldn't be that far away.

Dani eased down, slipping beneath fronds of the nearest fern and a branch of wild berry vine to hide. She rested her elbows on the ground and brought her rifle up tight to her shoulder. Uncomfortable as heck, but she could bear it.

Another bark. Dani swung the rifle.

"Shh, Lottie. Please."

Bingo. This time Dani spotted him. Doug kneeled on the forest floor, clutching Lottie to his chest. He stroked the little dog's fur as she licked him all over the face and yipped. Dani couldn't take the shot without risking Lottie's life.

She didn't know what to do. Killing that little dog wasn't fair. Dani loved her. Melody loved her. She couldn't do that to Lottie. But she couldn't let Doug live, either. He'd tried to kill her. He'd blamed her for his sister's death.

"Set the dog down, Doug!"

Dani swiveled in alarm. She would recognize Colt's voice anywhere. Where was he? She scanned the trees to her right, searching for any sign of the man. Nothing.

He was concealed well. She turned back to Doug. He was doing the same, searching the woods for the source of Colt's voice. Clutching Lottie to his chest with one hand, he stood up with a handgun in the other. "This is all your fault!"

"No, it's not. Everyone had a choice. You made yours."

"Melody didn't deserve to die!"

"No, she didn't. But it was an accident."

"I wish you'd never stepped foot in Eugene!" Doug's voice grew more desperate with every word. It shook and trembled and his grip on Lottie tightened so much the dog yelped.

"Put her down!"

"No!" Doug jerked his head down to look at the dog, then back up to the forest. He brought his right hand with the gun up to Lottie and shoved the barrel into her chest. "I'll shoot her. I swear to God I will!"

"Just put her down and no one will get hurt."

Dani wished she were a better shot. If only she could take him out. But no way would she be able to hit Doug and not hurt Lottie. She didn't know what to do. All she could hope for was that Colt and Larkin had a plan.

Doug jerked the dog around and she whimpered.

"Last chance, Doug. Put her down."

"No!" Doug pulled back the hammer on the handgun.

Dani braced herself. Could Colt really do it? Could he really shoot Doug and miss Lottie?

"We'll let you keep the guns. Let the dog go and you can walk out of this forest with all the weapons and ammo a free man."

Doug turned around in a frantic circle, shaking his head as he held the gun on Lottie. He opened his mouth to speak, but Dani couldn't make out the words. She rose up out of the ferns and rushed forward.

"I'm sorry. I'm sorry, Mel. I have to do it. I'm so sorry."

His frantic mumbling sent Dani into a panic. She

rose up to her full height and exposed herself. "No! Doug if you're going to shoot anyone, shoot me!" She held her arms out wide as Doug lifted his head.

He moved his gun hand away from Lottie and Dani screamed.

CHAPTER THIRTY

DANI

A shot pierced the stillness.

Dani staggered back.

Doug crumpled to the forest floor.

No! She rushed forward, tearing through the brush to get to Lottie. The little dog lay on the ground, still and not moving. Dani dove for her, heedless of Doug's body a few feet away. She scooped Lottie up into her arms.

"Please be alive. Please." She stroked the little dog's fur and a tiny grumble rumbled up from her throat. Dani exhaled in relief as Colt thundered up to her side.

"What the hell were you doing?"

"Saving Lottie." Dani eased the little dog's fur away from her face and Lottie's little black eyes blinked. She might be in shock or injured, but Lottie was alive. She looked up at Colt. "Thanks for taking the shot."

He shook his head. "I didn't."

Dani's eyes went wide. "Then who did?"

Walter stepped out of the weeds and stopped beside Doug. He lowered himself into a crouch and felt for a pulse on Doug's neck. "I did. I wasn't sure about the truth of this feud until that moment." He stood up with a solemn frown. "You just don't kill a good dog."

Larkin arrived on the scene from the other direction, half-running, half-skidding down the hill. "I tried to come at him from the back, but I was too slow."

"It's all right." Colt tilted his head in Walter's direction. "He took care of it."

Larkin held out his hand and Walter shook it. "Thank you."

"You're welcome. Although the three of you owe me a new tent and some gear. Your friend here shot up my entire camp."

Colt nodded. "We owe you a lot more than that."

Lottie squirmed in Dani's grip and she bent to set the little dog on the ground. After a head-to-toe shake, Lottie scampered a few feet away, did her business, and rushed back to Dani's feet. She scooped her back up and smiled. "I think she's going to be okay."

"Thanks to Walter, so are you." Colt stared at her, his eyes clouded and expression severe.

Dani looked away.

At last, Colt turned to Larkin. "Help me dig another hole, will you?"

Larkin nodded. "I'll get the shovel."

Walter held his arm out for Dani. "I can take you back to camp. We can chop up venison for Lottie and clean that wound on your face."

Dani reached up to feel crusted blood covering her cheek. She swallowed. In the tumult of the shootout, she'd forgotten all about it. "Thanks."

Walter turned to Colt. "You all right here?"

"We are. Thank you."

Dani let Walter lead her away from Doug's body and back to camp.

She sat down next to the fire in the same spot she'd been in before the shooting happened. Lottie settled in on her lap, nuzzling her hand until Dani relented and stroked her fur. It didn't seem real.

Everyone they met in Eugene except for Larkin was dead. Two entire families wiped out because of what? Dani might have defended herself to Walter, but on the inside, guilt festered. She couldn't help but wonder if five people wouldn't be alive and happy if she hadn't wrecked their lives.

"Don't blame yourself." Walter crouched at her side with a wet rag.

She pinned him with a glare. "Why not? It's all my fault."

"You didn't kill Doug."

"I might as well have. He blamed me for Melody's death. He lost control because of me."

Walter dabbed at her bloodied cheek. "He had a choice out in those woods. Accept what happened and move on, or not. He chose not."

Dani winced as Walter pressed on the cut. "Colt and I should have left them alone. I thought about it so many times. I should have just disappeared even if Colt didn't come with me."

Walter stopped cleaning. "Don't think like that. You and Colt are family and you need to stick together."

Her brows knitted. "He's not my family."

Walter tilted his head. "Really? You might not be blood relatives, but that man looks at you the same way I look at my daughter. Don't discount his loyalty."

Dani swallowed. Colt thought of her as a daughter? She wanted to believe Walter, but the events of the past week had her all twisted up in knots. Harvey, Gloria, and Will were a real family and they were dead. Melody and Doug were siblings and they were dead.

Maybe a family wasn't the best thing to have.

Walter started up on her face again and she closed her eyes. "Do you miss your daughter?"

"Very much. And as soon as I've gathered enough food, I'll be headed straight back to her."

"Aren't you afraid something might happen to her while you're gone?"

He hesitated, the rag pressed against Dani's cheek as he thought it over. "No. The place is secure. I'm the one at risk."

She snorted. "Because of us."

"Not only you. I've got food. Supplies. Anyone could come along and try to take what I have."

Dani opened her eyes. "We could help you. Provide security and hunt."

Walter smiled. "That's a nice offer."

"It's not a bad one, either." Colt emerged from the forest, dragging a sled loaded down with all sorts of gear. Larkin followed, burdened by three black duffel bags caked in dirt.

"We've got enough guns and ammunition to arm an entire town." Larkin dumped the bags in the middle of the clearing. "Maybe we could come to an arrangement."

Walter stood up as Larkin unzipped the bags. He walked over and inspected the contents. "Where did these come from?"

"The Camaro that killed the Wilkins family. The driver was a transporter."

Walter stepped back. "So they're stolen."

Colt tilted his head. "More like recovered."

"Do you know who they belong to?"

"Not for sure." Larkin rolled his shoulders to relieve the ache of the bags as he explained. "The men I was running from when you found me came looking for them. But we don't know if it was an arm's length transaction or if they already owned the weapons."

Colt eased the sled to the ground and set to work unhooking the netting and poles. "The two men were Cunningham's thugs."

Walter stilled. "You stole from Cunningham?"

"We stole from a dead man in a Camaro. We don't know if he was part of Cunningham's crew or not."

Walter turned back to Dani. He stared at her like she was the decision point in some internal battle she didn't understand. Who was Cunningham and what did he have to do with any of this? She chewed on her lip as Walter exhaled. Was he going to let them stay? Could they trust him?

"All right. You all can stay. But only until I've gathered what I need. Then we go our separate ways."

Colt stuck out his hand as Walter turned back to face him. "Deal."

Walter shook it and Colt set to work unpacking the gear from the Humvee.

Larkin grabbed a shovel and headed toward a semi-concealed spot beneath a tree branch. "Can we agree there's no digging tomorrow? I'm tired of digging." He stabbed the ground with the shovel and lifted a chunk of dirt and forest debris.

Dani watched Larkin work as Walter came back with a blob of goop on his finger. He smeared it on her cheek. "There might be a shard of that mug still in there. After the inflammation dies down, I can take a look. Then we can stitch it up."

She nodded.

Walter patted her knee. "I'll relight the fire and make some tea. I think you need it."

Dani swallowed. Every muscle in her body ached. Her cheek throbbed, her knees were bruised from where she fell to the ground when Doug started shooting, and she wanted nothing more than to curl up and forget the past week ever happened.

But she couldn't. That was another difference between now and before the power grid failed. Back then, if you didn't like something, you could ignore it.

Bury it behind a television screen or a fancy phone. She thought about Will and his refusal to accept the changed world. He tried so desperately to cling to the comforts of before: battery-operated video games and a computer that wouldn't turn on.

Out in the forest, with nothing to remind them of high-rises and offices and the constant hum of electronics, they were forced to face their fears. Decisions had a way of sticking around now, for good or bad.

Walter crouched in front of the fire and Dani twisted to face him. "If you want us to leave, it's okay. We can go."

He glanced up in between nudging the kindling beneath the wood and pulling out a lighter. "I've made my choice. You all can stay."

"We might be bad luck."

"I'll take my chances."

"We could end up getting you killed."

Walter lit the kindling and blew on it in slow, measured breaths until the wood caught. He leaned back, resting his hands on his thighs. "A branch from the tree over there could crack and take me out in an instant. This fire could spark and spread through the forest in an instant. One of the animals I kill could have a disease that drags me under."

He stood up. "There's a million ways I could go every day, Dani. I know the odds."

The ghosts of the people dead because of her filled her vision. "I don't want to get you killed."

Walter's face eased into a smile. "I've survived a hell

of a lot worse than sharing a camp with a former SEAL, an army officer, and a teenage girl who's as brave as any Marine. We'll be fine."

Dani swallowed. "So whatever happens next?"

"We'll be in it together."

DAY THIRTY-NINE

CHAPTER THIRTY-ONE

COLT

Northern California Forest
6:30 a.m.

Colt eased a breath from his lungs in a slow, measured stream. The marshes around the edge of the pond held more ducks than a man could eat in a lifetime. He eased into a crouch just outside of the water's edge. Lottie sat beside him, alert and waiting.

The first hint of a call sounded in the distance and Colt readied his shotgun. A V of five birds swooped low and circled. Colt waited. As they came in for a soft landing, Colt fired. One fell into the water and Lottie took off like a miniature torpedo.

The rest of the flock took to the air, squawking and carrying on. Colt stood up and waited. Five minutes later, a soaked little Lottie came swimming back with a bird twice her size in her teeth. Never in his life did he think a five-pound dog bred to fit in a purse would turn into a ferocious little hunter. But Lottie loved to retrieve.

She dropped the duck at his feet and shook her whole body from nose to tail. Water droplets flew everywhere and Colt fished a piece of jerky from his pocket. He fed it to the little dog, patted her head, and picked up the duck. By the time they made it back to camp, everyone else was awake and starting the day.

Dani crouched in front of the fire, getting it going just how Walter taught her. Larkin stood at the smoker, tending to the deer he'd killed the day before. Walter rummaged through their growing supply of dried plants and roots.

All together, they made an efficient four-person team. It wouldn't be long before Walter amassed everything he needed and then some. Colt hoped when the time came, Walter would decide to bring them all along.

He set the duck down on the prep table they had fashioned out of cut branches and walked over to Dani. The wound on her cheek was healing well, and thanks to Walter's even stitches, might not leave too jagged of a scar. Every day that went by away from Eugene and without conflict, Dani brightened. Gone were the pensive stares and somber moments when Colt wondered if she would ever laugh again.

If they could find some stability in this ever-changing world, she had the potential to grow into an amazing adult. Colt crouched beside her. "So what's on the menu today?"

She smiled. "Miner's lettuce, chicory root coffee, and guess what else?" Her eyes glittered as she waited.

"Deer jerky?"

"Nope."

"Duck meat."

"Try again."

"Smoked trout."

Dani laughed. "Eggs! Walter found a nest of quail eggs!"

"Don't get too excited. They're small and we only have four."

Colt grinned at Walter. "Now if we could just make some sausage, we'd be set."

"It's on the list. Find me some cloves and cayenne pepper and we're in business."

The tidy camp lapsed into silence as everyone went back to work. In no time, they'd put together a breakfast most people would have paid a premium for only a few weeks ago. He eased down to the ground beside Dani.

Walter sat at the makeshift radio station Larkin rigged up the day before. Thanks to the Humvee's battery and some tinkering by Walter and the creative use of the netting poles, they were able to not only receive radio frequencies, but broadcast as well. He cleared his throat, moved a few knobs and began his morning broadcast.

"Good morning. The time is 7:30 Pacific Standard, and it has been thirty-nine days since the United States power grid failed. My name is Walter Sloane."

He glanced over at Dani and smiled. "If this is your first time listening to my broadcasts, welcome. We have been through some of the most trying times we've ever had to face as a country. But we will persevere. If you are out there listening this morning, that means you are a survivor. You have found a way to keep going when the odds were stacked against you. Don't give up now. Together, we can weather this storm."

Dani leaned against Colt as Walter kept talking, describing the things people could do to find water or food. She couldn't help but wonder what Walter's own family was doing now. Were they listening to him? Did they know he was safe? Sooner or later, Walter would head back to them, and Colt, Dani, and Larkin would need to find their own way.

But for now, they were safe in the woods. With shelters made from Douglas fir and beds of matted pine straw, they were comfortable at night. Daily hunting and gathering provided enough to eat. The nearby creek gave them all the water they could ask for. It wasn't a home in a good neighborhood with a manicured lawn and a new car in the driveway. It was better.

Walter continued and Colt sat back to listen.

"Over the past week, I've learned that family isn't what's written on your birth certificate or determined by your last name. It's about finding like-minded people to share life's burdens. People you can trust. Yes, we're faced with challenging times, but don't let adversity stop you. Find others who want to survive and band together.

"You might not have much, but you're still breathing. You're still alive. So take in that next breath with hope and courage and optimism. This isn't the end of our country or our way of life. This isn't the end of you. It's a new beginning. Grab it with both hands and never let go."

Walter glanced at Colt before continuing. "I might not be broadcasting for a while after today, but don't worry. I'll be back before you know it. Until next time, this is Walter Sloane. Good luck." He clicked off the radio and exhaled.

Colt eased away from Dani as he addressed Walter. "So this is it?"

"It's time. Thanks to you all, I have more than I need and probably more than I can transport."

Dani shifted on the ground. "Wait, what's going on?"

Larkin picked at a pinecone. "Walter's packing up. He's going home."

"But…what about the camp and all the work we've put into it?"

Colt managed a sad smile. "We'll still get to use it."

Dani's gaze shifted from Colt to Walter as understanding spread across her face. "We aren't leaving."

"About that." Walter stood up and brushed off the dirt clinging to his pants. "What would you say about coming with me?"

"To your home?"

"It's not mine exactly. It belongs to another family. I don't know if they will accept you."

"But you're willing to bring us along?"

Dani clutched at Colt's arm. "I don't want to cause anyone else problems."

Walter nodded. "When we arrive, we'll explain the

situation and put it up to a vote. If it doesn't work, you all can go on your way or come back here."

Colt glanced at Dani. He thought about all she still needed to learn. All she would miss tagging along with two grown military men in the woods. He nodded. "Are there kids Dani's age?"

"College kids. Four or five years older."

Better than nothing. He reached out and squeezed her hand. "We'll come. And if it doesn't work out, no hard feelings."

Walter smiled. "Good. Because there's no way I can get there on my own."

Thank you for reading book six in the *After the EMP* series!

Book Seven will be coming to Amazon soon!

Looking for more *After the EMP* right now? You can find the rest of the series on Amazon.

If you haven't read *Darkness Falls*, the exclusive companion short story to the series, you can get it for free by subscribing to my newsletter:

www.harleytate.com/subscribe

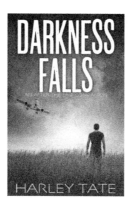

If you were hundreds of miles from home when the world ended, how would you protect your family?

Walter started his day like any other by boarding a commercial jet, ready to fly the first leg of his international journey. Halfway to Seattle, he witnesses the unthinkable: the total loss of power as far as he can see.

Hundreds of miles from home, he'll do whatever it takes to get back to his wife and teenage daughter. Landing the plane is only the beginning.

* * *

ACKNOWLEDGMENTS

Thank you for reading *Chaos Evolves*, book six in the *After the EMP* saga. I'm excited to merge the Darkness Trilogy and the Chaos Trilogy into one story for the next set of books in the After the EMP saga. Having Walter and Colt in the same story is a whole new adventure!

Thank you for coming with me on this survival journey. Although I try to be as realistic as possible, on occasion I take liberties with regard to actual places and things for the sake of the story. I hope you don't mind and can still go along for the ride!

Now that I am six books into this series, I've begun to think about additional stories I want to tell. If you have an idea for a new series (don't worry - I'm not leaving After the EMP just yet!), please let me know. I love hearing from readers.

If you enjoyed this book and have a moment, please consider leaving a review on Amazon. Every one helps new readers discover my work and helps me keep writing the stories you want to read.

Until next time,

Harley

ABOUT HARLEY TATE

When the world as we know it falls apart, how far will you go to survive?

Harley Tate writes edge-of-your-seat post-apocalyptic fiction exploring what happens when ordinary people are faced with impossible choices.

Harley's first series, *After the EMP*, follows ordinary people attempting to survive in a world without power. When the nation's power grid is wrecked, it doesn't take long for society to fall apart. The end of life as we know it brings out the best and worst in all of us.

The apocalypse is only the beginning.

Contact Harley directly at:

www.harleytate.com
harley@harleytate.com